The Deep

Prologue

Nice, France 1995

"If they see you, you're for it, Peter."

Fifteen-year-old Peter drew back from where he had sneaked a look through the open slit of the adjoining bedroom door and glared at his younger brother sitting up in bed, whose face registered the fear of the repercussions if caught by Jenny, their chaperon.

"Simon, when I come back I will knock three times, so make sure you are awake. OK?"

"Jenny will see you when you try to follow her, and she will tell Dad when he phones to ask how we are behaving," Simon countered, knowing that he already was an accomplice to his older brother's scheme. Dad would skin Peter alive should he find out he was out late at night on his own in a French town.

That his brother had the 'hots' for Jenny went without saying, always edging the adjoining bedroom door open when he thought that she might be changing.

Personally, he liked Sarah better, but Peter could just not keep his eyes off Jenny. His hands too if she would let him. How close his brother had come to having his face slapped he did not know, and deservedly so.

"She won't see me," Peter assured him. "Sarah has already looked in to make sure we are both asleep."

"But Jenny will be going to that grown up bar on the front. You'll get caught, then what will Mum and Dad say when Jenny or Sarah tell them? And I'll get into trouble for not telling. You wait and see."

"You're quite a little worm for eleven, Simon." Peter scowled at him contemptuously, crossing the room to the door that led out into the corridor, where he halted to look down at his brother sitting so apprehensively in bed. It was then he heard the girls' bedroom door open. "That's Jenny leaving. Now, remember, when I give three knocks open the door."

It was all a bit of a bind being able to leave your room but not having a card to get back in. So much for trust, he cursed.

"What if I'm asleep when you come back and I don't hear you?" Simon made a face, still worried by his brother's hair brained scheme.

"You better not be, you little toad. You can watch TV with the sound down to keep you awake. Now I must go."

Cautiously, the bigger boy opened the door a fraction and peered down the corridor where with a whir, the escalator had started its descent.

Peter gently closed the door and took off for the stairway, taking the steps two at a time in his haste not to lose his quarry on the off chance she might not head for Benny's, one of the bars on the sea front.

The foyer was busy that Saturday night when he reached it, although no one showed any interest in a teenager leaving the hotel at that time of night. Peter gave a little shiver, he should have put on a pullover over his T-shirt. Or was it the excitement of being out this late on his own, and following the girl he had come to fall in love with and whom he regarded as 'his girl' that had him shivering?

Peter gave another little shiver and this time he knew it was with excitement. Jenny had sat down at one of the outside tables in Benny's. He crossed the road and sat on a bench where he could watch her without being seen, and his heart skipped a beat in the knowledge that he could watch her every move without her being aware he was there. What would she do? Was she on a date? Peter seethed at the thought of someone else touching her.

When he'd first concocted the idea of following Jenny, it had been with the thought of taking her by surprise by sitting down beside her and telling her how much he loved her, and that he was not a little boy, and would prove it if she gave him the chance. No one need know, not even Sarah. Their love affair would remain a secret. But then he had reneged on the thought. What if she were to laugh at him; worse still, scold him for being out, and send him home, as a silly little boy? Tell Sarah so they could both have a laugh.

While these thoughts were surging through his mind, he saw the man sit down at Jenny's table. She smiled at him and they sat chatting for a while, touching hands. If only that had been him sitting there, Peter choked. Jenny laughed and sat back sipping her drink.

For the next half hour or so, the boy sat watching their every move, all the while his jealousy rose against the man talking to his girl. *Did this moron not know it was he who loved her?*

So what did it matter if Jenny was closer to this moron's age than he was? It was he who loved her, where as this person, he hesitated to say 'man', was only after one thing.

There was a scrape of chairs and they both rose. Now he would know what his girl was really like he thought, and started after them along the prom.

Jenny and her date strolled along the front until they came to one of the large yachts moored by the quayside. Jenny turned and Peter quickly ducked out of sight. When next he looked, they had gone on board. Taking a deep breath, he ran to where a light had suddenly shone out of a porthole and crouched down to peer inside, careful not to be seen.

Jenny was kissing the man who was gently lowering her on to one of the beds. Peter gulped. Had she met this guy before to let him do this to her? Now he was pulling her top over her head. Peter's breathing came faster, watching them undress until both lay naked. His ardour rose, his feelings a mixture of anger and excitement that it was not he who was making love to this beautiful girl. Yet, he could not bring himself to look away.

Peter was scarcely aware of making his way back to the hotel, visions of his girl making love to this man, whom she had just met, flashing through his mind.

Impatiently, he knocked on the bedroom door, angry at Simon taking so long to answer it, and burst into the room.

"Well, did you see her?" Simon sat excitedly on the top of the bedclothes, his eyes gleaming. "Did she go to Benny's?"

Angrily, Peter pulled off his top and hurled it across the room. "She did. And she did *meet* someone." He glared at his brother beaming up at him. "They made love, Simon, on one of the boats." His voice rose, choking his words. "They were naked, Simon!" He kicked out at his T –shirt. "Naked!"

His little brother's eyes widened. "What did she look like Peter? Did you see all of her? Was she beautiful?"

"Shut up, you little toad." Peter just did not care if Sarah heard him in the next room or not.

Offended by his brother's remark, Simon curled a lip. "Well you said all you ever wanted was to see her without her clothes on," he pouted, now wishing this brother of his had stayed at home.

"Well." It was Peter's turn to pout as he climbed into bed. "I'll let her know I saw her, not quite directly, but in a way that will have her guessing. Oh how she will know." Still seething, he pulled the bedclothes up to his chin.

"Did you have a good time last night?" Sarah set down the breakfast tray she had taken from the steward at the door. "Did you meet David again?"

"Yes to both your questions." Jenny gave a little laugh setting down the second tray on the table of their bedroom.

"Not that good, or you would be gushing to tell me." Sarah crossed to the adjoining room door and opened it. "Come on, you two. Up and at them, breakfast is here."

"Coming, Sarah," Simon yawned, sitting up and drawing a fist across his eyes.

"That goes for you too, sleepy head," Sarah addressed Peter's curled up figure. "You cannot be that tired. You did nothing all day yesterday but sit beside the pool. So come on, we have things to do."

Sarah turned from the door. "What's on today's agenda?" She drew her breakfast tray towards her.

"Better ask Bevis and Butthead in there," Jenny stifled a little yawn.

"Hard night, was it Jenny?"

The girls turned at the sound of the voice, where Peter stood in the doorway grinning.

"What would you know about hard nights?" Jenny scowled at him through her brows.

"Maybe more than you realise." Peter's grin widened.

The girls gave each other a look, implying that they did not understand what this little schoolboy was on about.

"What do you and Simon want to do today? As if I couldn't guess. Beach or pool?" Jenny gave the boy a steady look, daring him to contradict her.

"Neither." Peter took a step in to the room. "I want to take a walk to see the yachts," he said, toying with the salt shaker.

Jenny shook her head. "Not today, Sarah has too much to do, and it's her night off."

"Will she be going to Benny's?" It was Simon who had asked, having slipped quietly into the room, a mischievous grin on his young face.

Peter flashed him a warning.

"What's all this interest in yachts all of a sudden?" Sarah wanted to know, gesturing to the boys to start their breakfast.

The brothers gave a little laugh.

"Beats me what goes through their tiny minds." Sarah rose, and let out a sigh of resignation.

Chapter 1

Two weeks, I thought. I gave a sigh of contentment and sat down at a table a little way from the café entrance. Even under the table canopy, it was hot here in Nice, or did it just seem to be after the rigours of North Berwick? It was sunny there too, or least it had been when I left, with perhaps the cool breeze 'bouncing' off the Bass Rock making it that wee bit cooler. I took another satisfied look around at those already enjoying their Sunday morning coffee. I could get used to this, I thought, watching the waiter advancing briskly to take my order.

A sheet of white paper blew on to my table, and I put a hand out to stop its escape.

"Sorry for that. It belongs to me."

I looked to where a young woman from the next table had risen to retrieve her missive.

"In my day, it was a handkerchief the lady used to attract the young man's attention," I smiled.

"Don't flatter yourself mister," the owner of the Scot's voice assured me.

"I would not expect to, from someone with an accent like yours," I chuckled at the dark haired beauty.

I invited her to have a seat, which she did after retrieving her handbag and others things from her table.

"On holiday?" She drew her coffee cup towards her, righting her handbag which had toppled slightly.

"Two weeks. My brother Fenton joins me next week."

"Fenton?" The girl raised an eyebrow.

"Oh. Sorry. His name is Fenton Barns, and I'm his younger brother West, from North Berwick."

She offered a hand across the table. "I'm Sarah Donald, and I'm pleased to meet you Mister West Barns from North Berwick." She gave a little laugh as if having found something amusing.

"Are you here on holiday too?" I asked, hoping she would say yes, and that she too was on her own.

"If you call looking after one teenager and an eleven year old boy a holiday." She drew me a look.

"You can't be…"

"I'm not their mother, numpty." Sarah shook her head despairingly.

"No I didn't think you were," I apologised, thinking this lassie doesn't mince her words.

"Jenny and I are looking after the poor wee souls until Mummy and Daddy arrive next week."

It was the way she had said it that told me they could be nothing other than two spoiled rich kids.

"A handful, are they?" I took a sip of coffee while waiting to hear all the woes of having to look after delinquents of the upper class. Instead, she surprised me by giving a slight shrug of her shoulders and adding. "They're not too bad, I suppose."

My lack of response had her continue. "Mr Desmond, their father, owns a construction business back home. We…that is I live with the family on the coast up Aberdeen way, that's if we are not on his estate in Florida."

She saw by my look that I was impressed, "I know, money talks." She smiled

"Talks to me too," I said. "It usually says goodbye."

"I'm his secretary when Peter and Simon are away at boarding school," she continued to explain, "but, at present, I am helping to look after them until both parents arrive next week."

"And Jenny?"

"Oh, Jenny comes from London. She's a student and is helping while the boys are on holiday from school. It requires two to look after those laddies. We have alternative evenings off. We need it I can tell you."

She drained her coffee and sat back in her chair, giving me the once over. I hoped she approved by what she saw, which was a slightly built man rapidly approaching thirty.

"What do you do to keep the wolf from the door, Mr Barns?"she said at length.

The last thing I wanted to admit was that I was a Private Investigator, which pre-empted the usual questions of how many murders might I have solved, as finding the odd cat and dog, unfaithful husband or wife, instead, never failed to dampen their enthusiasm, or to say the least, disappointment that I might not be as exciting to be with as James Bond. So instead I said with a shrug,

"I'm a car salesman." Now I was thankful that I had learned a little something of the trade from a friend.

"Must be quite exciting, you getting to drive all those new fast cars. Lucky you." Sarah showed she was impressed.

"Lucky me?" I frowned.

Sarah made a face. "Not so exciting then?"

"I can safely say I haven't sold many cars."

"Never mind, I'll get Mister Desmond to buy a fleet of them when next he's in North Berwick." She gave her watch a glance which appeared to tell her that it was time to leave this dull car salesman. "It's my night off, so I have a few things to do before then."

My heart gave a little skip. "If you haven't anything arranged for tonight, will you have dinner with me?"

"You're a fast worker, Mr Barns." She looked amused, and got up. "I suppose that's your car sales training?"

"Not quite. But I only have a few days before my brother arrives."

She thought for a moment before eventually answering. "Well I suppose that would be nice. We leave next week ourselves. Do you like Chinese?

"As a Race, their quite clever," I said, pretending not to have understood the question.

She laughed. "Pretty funny. You know what I mean, for a Chinese meal."

"Providing I don't have to use chopsticks."

"You find them difficult?"

I nodded. "Especially with tomato soup."

"You are quite funny…for an Eastie that is."

"Unlike you Weegies who are full.."

"Now now, Mister West Barns," she gently scolded me.

"I was going to say full of wit, or something similar."

She laughed and shook her head. "I think we should leave it there, don't you think? Do you know of a place called Benny's on the front?"

"No. But I will find it."

"Good, 7.30 suit you?"

"You bet," I said.

It was then as she put out her hand to pick up her bag that another hand got there first and, in one swift movement, had snatched up the bag and was off amongst the coffee tables before I could say ' oh dear,' or something to that effect.

I jumped to my feet an eye on the departing figure, for to lose sight of him now would be fatal.

It was times like these that the slight disablement to my leg which had me pensioned from the Force told and in no small way. However, with the thought of becoming a hero in the eyes of my lovely new acquaintance, I spurred myself on. Fortunately for me, but not the fugitive, a waiter stepped out of the cafe doorway, the collision sending his laden tray crashing to the ground, and me time to get closer to establish that it was a teenager that I was chasing.

Recovering from his unexpected encounter with the waiter, my young fugitive rounded an empty table next to the kerb and was halfway across the busy road before I reached it. I followed and was almost knocked down by a car, having forgotten that traffic here drove on the wrong side of the road, and I signalled the driver my apologies as I polished his bonnet with my posterior while passing in hot pursuit.

Aware that I was still chasing him, the youngster increased his speed and thereby his intent to lose me, which he almost did by dodging up a side street and I lost him momentarily amongst the stalls and people it would seem intent on aiding him by hindering my process, my effort finally forcing me to halt and recover my breath and give my aching legs a rest.

While I stood there, my head almost at my knees and fighting for breath that he saw me and turned up an alleyway. I followed, but it was no use, I just had to stop again and, still gasping for breath, I took in the empty space before me. He had disappeared.

I took in a great gulp of fresh air, my eyes travelling from doorway to doorway and I cautiously moved forward, expecting at any time to see him dash out of one of them. There was nothing, only the sound of traffic in the street behind me.

Here, I was in another world with thoughts running through my mind that this guy might not be alone. I took a few steps closer to what appeared to be a narrow alley and peered into its dark interior. Something white caught my eye and I looked up to see a pair of shorts from which dangled two dark brown legs in the act of clambering over a wall, and I ran as fast as my rasping breath would allow. It was now or never if I were to stop him. With one leg already hoisted on top of the wall, my thief was almost over, and I caught hold of his other leg and pulled, toppling him to the ground in a heap in conjunction with a few French oaths that I was sure no youngster should be emitting.

"Wee mongrel," I wheezed, grabbing him by the collar before he could get to his feet, and feeling my injured leg throbbing with this unusual activity.

The teenager looked up at me and held out Sarah's bag by way of a peace token. "Please, monsieur." His dark brown eyes stared into mine and I saw nothing other than regret. Somehow, this regret seemed real, not one that I had witnessed in the Force when regret was nothing other than at having been caught.

For a moment, we stood there, the boy's dark eyes weighing up the repercussions of what he had done. "I will not do it again," he pleaded in broken English.

"Not to me you won't, you young sod." I gave him a slap which I thought I was entitled to, considering the pain I was in. "But what other poor sod will you do it to?"

I could see he did not understand me, for he just stood there studying his trainers as if seeing them for the first time and wondering how they had got there, and I smiled at my own humour for no one else would, especially Ali Baba here.

I took Sarah's bag and jerked a thumb in the direction of the alley's entrance. "Bugger off."

He did not seem to understand but just stood there awaiting my next move and with it his fate. "Go..Aller!" This time my expression and thumb did the trick. With what I thought were a few words of thanks, and a polite bow, he was gone quicker that my week's retirement pension.

Softy, I said to myself. *Just because you have met a pretty face you have let him off the hook,* though in reality I just could not bring myself to face all the hassle of involving the Gendarme, especially if it was to interfere with my date for the evening.

The Hotel Grande overlooked the beach and was definitely up market to my own, which had a sea view if you owned a pair of binoculars, and a compass.

Meeting Sarah that evening past had been a delight, when once more she had thanked me for returning her bag, which she said had contained all of her credit cards together with a fair amount of cash. She was only too willing to reward me, but being a gentleman, I had of course, refused, there being other ways (although not quite so gentlemanly) I had in mind in which she could reward me.

The evening had passed pleasantly enough, although a bit dicey when I began what I thought would be an amusing anecdote as a Private Detective until I remembered that I was supposed to be a car salesman and had to extricate myself before I choked in my own deceit. To my surprise, Sarah had agreed to meet me again next morning and had proposed her hotel, so here I was knocking apprehensively on her door. After a few seconds, it opened but not to the girl of my desire but a brunette, which had me thinking I had chosen the wrong door.

"Sorry. I was looking for Sarah Donald," I began.

"Yip, she's here. Come in." The brunette charmer turned to let me follow her into the room, or suite rather, for this room was large, with a kitchen bar, TV, small tables, and plush chairs dotted around the walls, and my mind went back to what Sarah had told me about 'daddy' and his construction company.

"If you want to see the yachts, you better get a move on, I haven't all day." Sarah appeared out of the adjoining room. She saw me and smiled. "So you found us?"

"I'll bet he wishes he hadn't when he meets those two." Jenny jerked a thumb in the direction of the boys emerging from the adjacent room.

I smiled what I hoped would stand for a contradiction. "Oh I don't know. They look harmless enough."

"Fool." Jenny threw her eyes heavenwards.

"This is Peter, he is the elder." Sarah introduced the taller of the brothers.

"Pleased to meet you, Peter," I said offering my hand and had it shaken by a boy with thick jet black hair.

"I told you he was a fool," Jenny sighed.

"Please to meet you, Sir." The boy said and stood back a little to let his younger brother introduce himself.

I gave a chuckle, and shook the hand of a fair haired boy whose clear blue eyes shone up at me, and I had the feeling that this little one could be much more than a handful despite his good manners, and angelic appearance.

"The boys want to walk round the yachts. I hope you don't mind?" Sarah asked, and I saw that she really wanted me to say that I didn't in the least mind.

Jenny picked up her tote bag, and gave a sigh. "I don't know what all this interest is, in yachts all of a sudden."

"Don't you Jenny?" Peter threw his brother a conspiratorial look, and turned away to hide his grin, and I was immediately suspicious that these two had more than an elbow up their sleeves, that is if their T-shirts had any sleeves.

"There's one big yacht I'd like you to see Mr Barns," Peter addressed me. "It's called The Sea Horse." He threw the brunette a look, gauging her reaction, then a grin at his brother, and I knew there was something going on between these two cherubs.

Jenny sucked in a breath and quickly countered, "Ok, smart guy, let's go and see this yacht of yours."

We left the hotel, eventually walking past Benny's where later after our 'chopstickless' Chinese meal, I had spent the evening with Sarah.

"Nice bar that, Simon. When you grow up, you will meet all sorts of people there." Peter nodded at the bar.

I saw the boy flick a quick glance in Jenny's direction which enforced my conviction that he was baiting the girl in some way, although she herself appeared ignorant of any innuendo.

After a short walk, we arrived where the Sea Horse unlike most of the other yachts was anchored broadside to the quay.

"Is this it?" Sarah asked, drawing up to admire the luxury craft.

"Sure is, Sarah," Peter beamed. "Lots of exciting things can happen on a boat like this."

At last, I saw a flicker of realisation cross Jenny's face, quickly followed by a look of sheer anger at the older boy.

"It's smashing!" Simon gave a little skip towards the lowered gangway.

"Don't get too close, Simon," Sarah warned, taking a step or two forward.

"He'll be all right, lady."

I looked up to where the voice had come from. There, a big bearded man close on middle age stood leaning on a rail looking down at us, a cigar firmly gripped between his teeth.

"Would you like to come on board?" His question, I judged to be aimed more at Simon than the rest of us.

"Yes Sir. Please Sir." Simon's eyes shone with delight."

"Don't annoy the man, Simon," Sarah scolded her minion, placing a restraining hand on his shoulder.

"He's not annoying me lady." The man took the cigar out of his mouth and swept a hand at us. "Why don't you all come on board? See how the other half live so to speak." He let out a bellow of a laugh at his joke and wiped cigar ash off his white shirt.

"Can we, Sarah?" Simon looked up eagerly at the girl, who in turn looked at her companion.

Jenny gave a shrug. "Could do no harm, I suppose."

Simon did not await further confirmation before he was running up the gangway, turning to hasten his brother aboard. "You too, Mr Barns!" he shouted to me.

"Seems as though you have been Press Ganged into it, West." Sarah turned to laugh at me.

"As long as it remains tied up, or I jump ship at the first ripple of a wave."

"A land lubber, are you?" The big man asked watching me cautiously make my way on board. He held out his hand, "Walt Shawman," he introduced himself.

"Pleased to meet you, captain." I found myself shaking a very firm hand.

Shawman laughed. "I'm not the Captain."

"If you're not the Captain, will you not get into trouble for letting us come on board mister?" Simon peered up at the man, now clearly worried by his action.

The big man guffawed again and shook his head. "Don't rightly think so, as I own this darned thing." The accent was clearly American.

We all let out suitable noises of astonishment and, in my case, envy, not at his owning the craft but at the money involved, and, at the same time, calculating how many missing dogs and husbands I would have to find to pay for this little lot.

Shawman threw the stub of his cigar overboard and gestured to us. "Come below and have a drink…Coke for you two," he warned the boys with a laugh.

It was as we made our way along the passageway that we met the man in the purple suit with matching tie. Not only did he look out of place but his suit did as well, especially in this hot weather.

"I will be with you shortly, Raymond. Just letting these good folks have a look see over the old tub," Walt addressed the man, who gave a quick nod and disappeared into one of the cabins.

"Nice suit," Sarah whispered to me, a gleam in her eye.

"Don't knock it, that's my uniform for selling cars," I whispered back.

Below deck could only be described as opulent, especially the salon he ushered us into.

A steward appeared out of nowhere and took our orders, the boys scarcely able to contain their excitement at being on board.

Simon stared out of a porthole turning to ask excitedly, "When will you be going out to sea, Mr Shawman?"

"Mind your manners young man, and don't be so nosey," Jenny scolded him.

Shawman chuckled at the reprimand. "Tomorrow on the tide. Would you like to come on board?"

Simon's eyes almost popped out of his head, staring first at the big man, then at his brother, then back to the girls. "Could we, Sarah? Jenny?" The questions came gushing out at this the greatest thing that had ever happened in his young life.

"Your mum and Dad will be here next week, and they might not want you gallivanting all over the ocean," Sarah pulled a face.

"We will only be gone a few days or so. I aim to do a bit fishing then be back here for a business conference. I have to pay for this old tub somehow." The big man lifted his drink letting the girls think it over.

"Please, Sarah." This time, it was Peter who did the pleading.

"Perhaps we could, Sarah," Jenny said, looking at her fellow worker. She turned to Shawman. "I see no problem if it is only for a couple of days or so."

"You have my word gal. Back here Saturday …Sunday, at the latest. You can phone the kids' folks to confirm that it is all Ok if you have a mind?"

Sarah shrugged her resignation. "I suppose it will be all right, but first we will have to inform Mister Desmond of our intentions."

"I love you Sarah," Simon ran and put his arms around the girls waist.

"Well that will be a first," Jenny laughed.

"That's settled then be here four o'clock tomorrow morning. We sail on the tide." He turned to me. "You too, Mister Barns, should you have a mind."

It was what I feared. I wanted to spend some time with Sarah but the thought of going out to sea frightened me all the way to the bottom of Davy Jones' locker. A slight swell was all it took to have me leaning over the side and sharing my breakfast with any passing fish. Yet, what else would I do until Fenton arrived, if not in the company of a pretty face, or in this case two pretty faces? And, so it was, although unknown to me at the time, that I came to make the most fateful decision of my life.

"Ok. I'll give it a go. But don't expect me to splice the main brace or whatever you sailor types get up to at sea." I saw the look of pleasure on Sarah's face. At least, I thought, I will have someone to hang on to as I quietly pass away. At least, Fenton would not have the pleasure of dancing on my grave as he jokingly said he would, should I be buried at sea. Or would the big mutt find some way of foiling me by turning up in a rubber dinghy?

Chapter 2

I met the boys and girls next morning at the pre-arranged time, and together we set off for the yacht. The boys were ecstatic at their forthcoming 'ocean voyage': me, not so, and still yawning at this early hour. In fact, I had mulled over my decision most of the previous evening wondering if Sarah was worth the risk of my drowning, or becoming shark bait, although a shark would have to be pretty acrobatic to catch me up in the crows nest, that's how close I meant to be to the sea.

Walt Shawman was the first to greet us. "So you all decided to come." He gave the boys an encouraging slap on the back as they stepped on board, and Sadie and Jenny a warm smile, ushering us all below deck. "You can stow your gear down here." He opened a cabin door to reveal a two-bunk-cabin complete with all amenities, then much to my disappointment the one next door which I and the boys would share.

"I have the top bunk," Peter let out, scurrying to claim his sleeping quarters.

"You monster." Simon walked dejectedly to the bottom bunk, shooting hostile looks up his older brother, already lying, hands clasped behind his head in a gesture applying undisputed occupancy.

I myself had a double bed to myself on which I threw down my overnight bag, and hoped I had packed the necessary gear for this epic voyage. I also said a silent prayer that life jackets had been provided and within easy reach at all times.

I stepped back into the passageway where Walt was in conversation with a lean man with a dark complexion and I guessed a nature to match.

"This is your captain," Walt introduced the man to all of us gathered in the narrow passageway. "Meet Captain Henri Valleye, folks."

We all muttered our pleasure at meeting the man, whom I carefully studied in the hope of reassuring myself that he had a spotless driving licence, or the seagoing equivalent thereof.

"We must weigh anchor if we are not to miss the tide, Mr Shawman." The Captain's accent was unmistakably French.

"Very well, Captain." Shawman turned to follow the slim man to the upper deck, the boys pushing past me, determined to be part of what was going on.

Simon ran to where one of the crew was busy with a rope (which I later learned was called a line at sea) and the man shouted to him to take hold of an end, which he did with all the enthusiasm of a mid shipman of old. Meanwhile, his brother was busily engaged somewhere near the anchor

Sarah came to sit beside me. "Much the busy little sailors, are they not?" she laughed, watching Jenny pick up the boys discarded T-shirts from off the deck.

Jenny saw us, who, with a shake of her head, held up the shirts to us. "Two minutes and they are already part of the crew," she sighed. "Whatever next?"

"At least they are enjoying themselves," I said to Sarah.

"And you're not?"

I shrugged.

"I thought you said you lived in North Berwick, that's on the coast, isn't it? Don't you like the sea?"

"Oh it's a nice place all right. I wear St Michael pants but that doesn't make me Irish. To tell you the truth, the sea frightens the…out of me. I can't even swim. I sometimes get into difficulties paddling."

Sarah laughed. "So *why* did you come along?"

"To be near you." There, I had said it, now await reprisals.

"I thought as much West Barns. Gee you are easily pleased," she chuckled.

"I hope so," I grinned. Then we both turned our attention to the newest of crew members.

It did not seem too long before we had left the protection of the harbour and into the dangers of open water. Although to be fair so was the weather with only a gentle swell, which was enough to have me reaching for my sea sickness pills that I had bought by the ton.

I sat watching the industry of all on deck. One of the crew, who later I learned was named Marco, took it upon himself to show Simon the ropes (literally) whilst another crew member helped Peter climb the rigging, much to the concern of Jenny who was shouting up to him to come down, only to have her warning waved aside by a gesture of the boy's right hand.

"Cheeky wee monkey," Sarah seethed beside me. "He has the hots for her, you know," she explained. "Can't take his eyes off her. His hands too, if she would let him. He'll be a handful with the girls when he gets a wee bit older and realises how good looking he is."

Secretly, I admired the boy's good taste, even although my preference was for the girl sitting beside me.

How long ago was it when, although lacking the boy's looks I had been as active as he? Now, with a semi-gammy leg, it took me all my time to kick a ball, or run round to the shops. My only consolation was that I did not have a limp that showed.

Lazily, I watched a head, then the shoulders appear from below deck. The head turned in my direction, let out a gasp, then froze. It was my erstwhile handbag thief. Also taken aback by this unexpected encounter, I stared back, swallowed and regained my composure. I nodded in a way that suggested that we had never met, and beside me Sarah greeted the boy with a smile and a cheery hello sailor. Evidently, she did not recognise him.

Clearly relieved, the boy turned away to his duties.

"Nice looking kid," Sarah commented, watching him climb the rigging.

"That's me dumped then." I let out an exaggerated sigh of resignation.

"A bit young, but next voyage you never know…you never know." She tilted her head back, a hand held up to shade her eyes, watching the boy's progress.

"I'm too young for you this voyage, am I ?" I emitted a sound of disbelief.

"Not you numpty, him up there!" she pointed to the mast that the boy was climbing.

She saw me grin. "Moron," she admonished me, with a dig to my ribs.

Suddenly, the yacht gave a lurch and I saw Peter grab the rigging. Then, with his free hand, point to where a white launch, the French tricolour, painted at an angle by the bows was heading towards us.

Shawman came up from below, saw the launch, then turned in our direction. "Coastguard," he said simply.

Sarah and I rose and walked to the rail where the launch was coming alongside, already interested in what was taking place.

"Monsieur Shawman!" the French captain called out pleasantly "After the big fish as usual?"

"Yip. Do you want to come on board? Sip a wine or two?"

"Thank you but no, monsieur, we are already overdue in port. I think we can trust you by this time. Ok"

Shawman smiled and waved an understanding. "Maybe next time."

The French officer waved back. "Have a good trip." He swung his attention to the rest of us, and Shawman shouted across to him, "my extended family."

"Oui monsuer. And you too Captain Valleye," he called out, the Captain having joined his employer by the rail. Then, the Coastguard was gone, churning up the sea in its wake.

Sarah left me to talk to Jenny and I caught sight of our young miscreant watching me. He made his way to where I stood, and leaned on the rail, his eyes on the departing boat.

"You did not tell them? Why not? You could have had me arrested, as would Mister Shawman had he known what I had done."

I shrugged. "Everyone deserves a second chance."

"I could have told you I stole because my mother is sick…dying of cancer, but that would not have been true. Or that my father is a drunkard who beat me so badly that I had to leave home. This, Monsieur would also not have been the truth."

I turned to face him. "Then why did you do it?"

At first he did not answer, but just stood there his eyes on the far horizon.

"The people I owe rent to are not so very nice, and I only work for Monsier Shawman when Sea Horse is in Nice, so I am not so well off. Oui? See." He held out his arm to show me a knife scar about six inches long. "Next time they say it will be my face."

"And you need your looks for the mademoiselles. Is that it?" I smiled, letting him know that I understood.

Further down the deck, Simon and Marco were enthusiastically hauling in some rope. Simon waved and I waved back. "I think that little matelot could do with a hand," I nodded, and the boy turned his head to see what I meant.

"Merci monsieur. I will not forget your kindness." He made to move away.

"Ok you do that. What's your name by the way?"

"Jacques."

"Mine is West. So back to work with you Jacques."

"Consorting with the crew are we Mister Barns?" Sarah chuckled on her way to my side.

"It pays to know someone who knows where the life jackets are kept," I replied in mock seriousness. "For you never know, you never know." I winked.

That evening, a man of about my own age came to join us at dinner.

"This is David...David Mason," Walt introduced him. "He is second in command of my little tub," he explained.

Mason acknowledged us each in turn. "I hope you enjoy our little cruise. It certainly will be if the skipper here catches what he is after."

"I thought Mr Shawman wasn't the Captain?" Peter asked, drawing the salad bowl towards him.

"I only used the word loosely, kid," David winked.

"Where *is* Captain Valleye?" Shawman asked. "I thought he was joining us."

"He says some stormy weather is coming up. Though not too much to worry about." David took the bowl from the boy, who drew him, at what I could only describe as a look of sheer hatred, though I didn't know why.

Sarah threw me a mischievous look to find out how I was taking the news about the weather, which was, in my case, badly.

"Will we have to go up the mast to fix the sails if there is a storm?" Simon looked excitedly around him at the prospect.

Walt let out a guffaw and sat back sipping his wine. "It won't be that bad, young matelot," adding at the youngster's look of disappointment, "though you can spend the night in the Crows Nest and keep a lookout for Moby Dick, should you have a mind."

"Have a whale of time," Jenny tittered.

"Oh Jenny," Simon pouted, realising he had been the brunt of the joke.

Walt lit up his cigar, inhaled and said, "Should you wish to phone home, you better do it now, cell phones won't be of much use from here on in, especially if there is a storm brewing. So if you have any last requests?"

Sarah exploded in laughter at my expression as I threw my eyes heavenward, silently wishing she had been an ugly old sea wart and I would not be in this predicament now.

"You're alarming Mr Barns," Sarah tittered. "He can't swim you know."

"Thank you very much oh siren of the ocean," was all I could think of saying in defence of my masculinity, staring at her across the table.

"No worries, West. It doesn't matter if you can swim or not, the difference is only a few minutes," David informed me seriously.

"Very comforting to know, David," I replied with a sigh.

"You can hold on to me, Mr Barns," young Simon reassured me with a nod. "I won't let you drown."

"Thanks kid. But how can you do that when you're up in the Crows Nest looking out for Moby Dick?" I raised an eyebrow at him.

"Oh you know they were only kidding me," Simon shook his head at what he saw was an ill conceived joke.

"On that score, I think we should leave it at that," Jenny interceded. "It's about time for you two bunking down, or words to that affect,"

"Oh Jenny," came a duo of protests.

I rose with the boys. "If I am to meet Davy Jones in his locker, then I think I should inform my brother Fenton," I advised them in mock seriousness. "Tell him he can have my Beano and Dandy books."

"Wait and I'll come with you, Admiral Nelson." Sarah made her way around the table to my side.

Standing on deck, I gripped the rail tightly, staring across the dark blue ocean, apprehensive of what lay beneath that huge expanse of water.

"Makes you quite humble when you look at it." Sarah pushed back a strand of black hair.

"Makes me quite feart," I said solemnly.

"It seems to go for ever."

"Just like Fenton when I won't buy him a drink."

Sarah appreciated the quip. "Must be quite a character."

"He is. Then again, so are a lot of polis," I said enjoying using my native dialect.

"You didn't tell me your brother was a policemen." Sarah turned to study my face.

"Sorry. I thought I did."

"Is he high up?"

"Only when he goes to the cafeteria on the fifth floor." She gave me a look which had me apologising and explaining that he was a Detective Inspector.

The girl gave a little shiver at a sudden breeze, and I took the double courage to let go of the rail and put my arm around her.

"That's better." She drew closer, and I knew I had made the right decision to come along. "Pity there's not a place where I can say, wait until I slip into something more comfortable."

"Last time a woman said that to me, she came back wearing a pair of Hush Puppies." I sighed.

I gave her neck a little peck and she drew back a little to stare up at me.

"Is that the best you can do?"

"Fair go," I said, "give me time to find my sea legs."

"Ok Mr West Barns, but it's not a world cruise we are on."

The boys were up and showered and scarcely able to contain their excitement at being at sea. I sat up yawning while they chose a T-shirt and discussed the dangers of wearing one that might not meet with either girls' approval. Eventually, the suitable attire chosen, they turned their attention to me.

"You'll miss breakfast Mr Barns," Simon warned me in a tone that boded disaster should this be the case.

Surprisingly, the pills seemed to be doing the trick, and in fact I was looking forward to my first meal of the day.

While I dressed, the boys discussed their sea chores for the day as laid down by Marco the night before. "You're really enjoying this trip, aren't you boys?" I gave each of them a grin.

"Oh yes, Sir, Mr Barns," both echoed.

I held up a hand. "I think we can dispense with the Mister or Sir. West will do. I'm not one of your schoolmasters, you know."

"No chance that you would be," Peter laughed. "They're all relics from the last War."

Peter apologised at the absurdity of the remark. "Well not quite," he laughed at me turning up my brows.

"Don't you like school?" I asked, lacing a shoe.

"Cairn's not too bad as schools go," Peter admitted, screwing up his brows. "It's the winter plays we have to put on for our parents that I hate most."

"Yes. This year it was a musical and none of us can sing," Simon moaned.

"Not the Sound of Music?" I laughed.

Peter shook his head. "Worse still, West Side Story of all things."

"I know what you mean," I nodded. "I took part in the sequel. It was called the Backside Story, and I played a bum." I had not long to wait for their response.

"Started at the bottom did you West?" Peter chuckled.

"I bet you made an ar…"

"That's quite enough from you Simon," Sarah suddenly warned from the doorway.

"Come on Peter, Marco will have us keel-hauled if we're late." Simon rushed to the door, squeezing past Sarah, anxious to be out of range of further reprimands from the girl.

I shook my head, and got out of Simon's way.

"You've made quite an impression I see," Sarah chortled at their departing figures.

I shrugged. "Just my usual charisma. Surprisingly, they're not bad kids, as kids go."

"You sound surprised. Did you expect them to be snobs because they attend a boarding school?" Sarah gave me a look suggesting that I should be ashamed at having thought so. "Their Dad, Mr Desmond is a self-made man, he knows what it is to have come up the hard way. I should think he would want the boys to learn something about the world as it is, not what they believe it to be from the inside of schools walls."

"I stand suitably chastised." I bowed my head in mock shame.

Sarah burst out laughing at me standing there. "Come on numpty, or you'll miss breakfast."

After breakfast, we all made our various ways on deck. In my case, to a seat under the cockpit, and watched the boys carry out their sea duties with all the enthusiasm of seasoned Jack Tars.

Shawman was somewhere on the port side casting out what could only be described as a rod big enough to haul in Moby Dick or his cousin Dopy Mick.

Jenny lay on her front sunbathing, with Sarah further astern talking to one of the crew. David Mason appeared from below and crossed to squat down beside the bathing girl who turned her head and looked up at him her fingers still laced together. She said something and he complied by undoing her bra strap and spreading white suntan lotion on her back.

My eyes drifted to Peter standing in the lower rigging, he was not looking at the girl but at the man stroking her bare back, a look of sheer hatred on his young face.

At that moment, David caught sight of his captain, signalling to him and silently rose to meet him.

In an instant, Peter was off the rigging his bare feet silent on the wooden deck as he ran to where Jenny lay, and kneeling down, gently spread the liquid on her back.

At first, I was not aware of holding my breath at the youngster having taken over where his rival had left off, and Jenny oblivious to the change of masseur her eyes closed continued to lie there appearing to be enjoying the sensation. I swallowed, imagining the boy's hormones going into double time with every stroke. This, according to Sarah, was what he had yearned to do, to be touching his sweetheart.

Peter stroked lower, touching her bikini bottom, his fingers exploring a little under the material. Jenny turned her head to the side to chastise her masseur for his boldness when she saw who it was. With a shriek, she rose to her knees, her bra clutched tightly to her chest.

Instantly, Peter was on his feet and quickly backing away before the wrath of the girl, his eyes wide with the realisation of what he had done and the liberty he had taken. Suddenly, he stopped, anger replacing fear. "So it was all right for David to do it to you, but not me?" He shrieked at her. "The same as he did here in the yacht the other night. You didn't mind then, even when you were *naked*." All the hurt and humiliation had gone into those few words, each syllable aimed to hurt, to wound this girl who in his own young way he loved.

"So you saw...you followed me, you little..." Jenny's eyes blazed at the boy.

"What's going on?" Sarah appeared beside Peter, her expression one of bewilderment.

Snatching up a towel, Jenny rose to her feet. "Let him tell you...the little shit. I hope his father cuts him off by the goolies." She turned in my direction, and I thought nothing was ever going to be the same again. Here, you could not just get up and leave. Here, we were all in the same boat so to speak.

That evening, the boys ate their meal in the galley, while we adults sat at the usual table in the salon.

Walt Shawman threw down his fork in a gesture of satisfaction. "Compliments to the chef." He sat back and surveyed his guests. "There seems to have been some sort of lovers' quarrel out there, so David here tells me."

"Not exactly a lovers' quarrel, Mr Shawman," Jenny sounded bitter. "Just a kid that has the hots for me."

Shawman extracted a cigar from its case. "Can't say I can fault his taste, gal." He had said it as a compliment, hoping to lighten an already stilted conversation.

"Ch..." Jenny halted. She started again. "He's only a boy."

"Maybe, but, at his age, I was chasing my first love. I dare say you fellas here know what I mean." For some reason, Shawman's eyes fell on me rather than David or his Captain, the latter who sat eyes down in deep concentration of twiddling a spoon through his fingers.

Somehow I thought that I was expected to answer him. "Youngsters grow up fast these days Mr Shawman, perhaps fast foods have something to do with it." I smiled hoping to defuse the situation. Instead, it seemed to deepen it. "I mean," I went on, "he has known about the birds and the bees for a long time now I should say." I knew I was not doing a very good job of this, especially the way Jenny was glaring at me, who I suspected had expected me to back her up about Peter being no more than a boy.

"You think that he was old enough to take advantage of Jenny? Or did he think himself justified to do what he did because his father was her employer?" David looked daggers across the table at me, and I heard a gasp of disbelief from Sarah.

"Birds and bees, David, that's all it was. A young man's obsession for a pretty face." Sarah admonished David's theory with a tut tut.

I was about to add, probably the boy's first taste of honey, but thought better of it and held my peace.

"Well, que sera sera," Captain Velleye sighed, putting down his instrument of concentration. "Now if you will excuse, me I must fulfil my duties and prepare for our other little squall, shall we say." He rose and bemused by this unexpected humour, my eyes followed his retreating figure and laughter out of the door.

Later, strolling, or swaying rather, along the deck as the first sea swell hit our vessel and I hoped there was not more stormy weather to come either from in or out of our boat, I asked of Sarah, "That didn't go down too well what I said at dinner, did it?"

"I think Jenny was more taken by surprise than shocked at Peter." Sarah halted by the rail and gave a little chuckle. "I think she is more embarrassed by what she must have said to Peter believing him to be David."

I turned my back and leaned on the rail. "Now I understand what all that hinting going on between the boys for Jenny's benefit was all about. It was David Peter saw making love to Jenny here on the yacht."

Sarah made a face. "Jenny has met David a few times before that night. I don't think Peter knew of this, but he certainly saw them together the night he slipped out. So now you know why Peter dislikes David so much. Undoubtedly, he will also have told Simon. You know what boys are like."

"I have a good idea having being one myself," I grinned.

"Also I think she might have been worried that Mr and Mrs Desmond would have found out that their son was out of his room at that time of night." Sarah turned to me. "Although, technically it was me to blame as I was on duty so to speak and not her."

"What do you think will happen now?" My eyes roamed over this lovely girl and I wanted to get on with more important things in life such as making love or near as damn to it.

Sarah sighed and pushed herself off the rail. "I expect it will soon blow over and we will all get back to normal.

"I hope so, and the same goes for this weather too," I said, lifting my eyes to a leaden sky.

The blow hit me midriff and I let out a yell. Faintly in the dim light of the cabin I saw Peter standing at the foot of my bed. Still feeling the effects of the pain, I struggled on to my side and reached for the lamp.

"Sorry, Sir…West," Peter apologised. "I was on my way back from the toilet and climbing back into bed when the boat gave a lurch and I landed on top of you. Sorry."

I sat up blinking through the pain. The yacht gave another sudden lurch to the side, and Peter made a grab for his bunk.

"Are we sinking?" a little voice asked, and Simon sat up rubbing the sleep from his eyes. He stared at us. "Will I get the life jackets?" His eyes were void of any fear. To him, it was all part of the adventure.

I saw water slush across the floor and let out an oath before I had realised it. "We *are* sinking," I shouted and got out of bed in one bound.

Peter laughed at my panic. "It's the head that's come off the shower, and the waters spilling onto the floor. I thought I had it sorted but evidently the head's come off again," he explained.

Something like my own, I thought, with a sigh of relief that we were still afloat. My stare flew to the porthole and the raging sea beyond. I never should have come, drowned, a result of a pretty face. How long could a few inches of steel hold back the might of an ocean? Had not the Titanic gone down by hitting an iceberg and I didn't mean a lettuce either. Then again, there were not many icebergs around the Rivera, yet knowing my luck there was always the odd chance.

Simon extracted himself from his bedclothes and stood up in time to introduce his head to my stomach when he fell.

"What's with you two? Have you got it in for me?" I gasped, rubbing where the recent cranium had indented my stomach.

"Sorry…West." Simon sat back down with a thump. He tried to rise, no doubt anxious to find where the lifejackets were kept and I was inclined to help him when he hit the side of the bunk. The wee boy let out a yell, and held his nose, and I imagined that I too had felt the impact of the blow.

Peter went to his brother's aid. "Your nose is bleeding, Simon."

I got a handkerchief from my trousers by the bedside and handed it to him. "Hold this under your nose and we'll get the girls to help you. They will know what to do." I guided him to the door and helped him hold his hankie.

Peter drew back. "I'll wait here." He hesitated and pointed to the bathroom. "I'll try and fix the shower again."

"Ok." I knew that he didn't want to face Jenny after their earlier altercation, so there was no point in arguing with him.

Holding the hankie in place as best I could, I helped the boy to the next door cabin where the girls were. I knocked and waited.

A few seconds later, the door opened to reveal Sarah standing there in a flimsy nightdress. I swallowed hard at what I was seeing. If only the circumstances had been different and we weren't sinking, I thought.

"What's happened?" Horrified, she looked at me, then at the boy with the blood now streaming down his bare chest.

"He bumped into his bunk when the boat gave a lurch," I explained.

Jenny appeared beside her friend. "You better bring him in." With one hand holding the hankie, and the other on Simon's shoulder, she ushered him inside.

"I'll wait out here. I hate the sight of blood."

"Coward," Jenny rebuked me with a mock frown.

"What's going on?"

I turned at the sound of the voice and Walt Shawman standing there. Although it was after three in the morning, he was still fully clothed, and suddenly I believed that we might indeed be sinking.

"Is everything all right?" I was afraid he might prevent me or the girls from panicking by not telling us the whole truth.

"Yip. Worst of the little squall is over. You can go back to bed now."

"It's Simon, he hit his nose on the bunk. That's why I am here." I tried to sound as though I had not been in the least worried about sinking.

Simon looked up at me through his hand held hankie, and I drew my eyes into slits daring him to say otherwise. His smirk was halted by Sarah tilting his head back and replacing the hankie with a wet cloth.

By morning, our little 'squall' was over and I surprised myself by actually eating breakfast, albeit a couple of croissants.

The crew were already on deck cleaning up what little damage the squall had done, and were quickly joined by my two cabin mates.

Swabbing the deck, Simon drew me a look which clearly stated 'coward', having remembered my reaction the previous night to our sinking.

"How's the nose?" I asked

He drew a finger down where, although it appeared to be bruised, it was otherwise undamaged. "Ok. A bit sore though."

"It's you that nose about it," I said with a chuckle.

Simon threw his eyes skyward. "Old folk," he sighed and turned away, relieved to be back at work and away from geriatrics and their daft puns.

By midday, we had dropped anchor, the sea calm as a mill pond, as the saying goes.

I took a stroll around the deck, the crew nowhere to be seen, probably below deck I thought enjoying a siesta out of the sun. I felt conspicuous in my shorts, and my white legs looked like two milk bottles, and I thought I must be the only completely white person on board. North Berwick's weather had a lot to answer for, I sighed, obviously the council had not signed up for Global Warming.

I drew close to the stern where Jacques was hard at work, his back to me and unaware that I was there. It was as he rose with something in his hands that the figure stepped out from behind the mast, lashing at the boy's bare back with a length of rope he was holding. The boy let out a cry, dropped what he was carrying and backed away as his attacker came at him again.

I rushed forward catching the tail end of the rope that he had raised to strike again, and jerked it out of the man's grasp before he was aware that I was there.

The man was big, twice as big and strong as me by the looks of him. Momentarily caught off balance, he staggered back his eyes blazing hatred, and out of the corner of my eye, I caught the look on Jacques face telling me that I should not have intervened and that I had only made things worse for him. Somehow, I was inclined to agree, but as they say on Mastermind I had started so I'll finish...one way or another.

Angrily, I threw the length of rope away. "The days of Blackbeard and his pirates are long gone, monsieur."

"You mind your business *monsieur.*" The retort was unmistakably Cockney. "You have no right to butt into matters that don't concern you. I discipline the crew around here."

He came towards me, intent on teaching me a lesson on how not to interfere. Now I knew the trouble I was in, much deeper I thought than that of the boy I had attempted to save. This man would have no hesitation on teaching me how to dive overboard.

He was almost an arms' length away when my hand found a belaying pin, and I hit him hard across the face. This thug I knew would not give me a second chance. He staggered back against the wooden railing, and momentarily caught off balance I hit him again and he went over the side.

"You should not have done that monsieur!" Jacques stared down at my adversary thrashing about in the water. "The Anglais will be most probably kill you for this." Jacques voice shook with fear. "Perhaps I should throw him a life belt? Make things a little easier."

Watching the man thrashing about in the water, and to hide my own fear and what repercussions my action might have, I said as calmly as possible. "Better if I should throw him an anchor to hold on to instead. What do you think Jacques?" I tried to make light of the situation but already my heart was pounding with what I had done.

"What the hell's going on?" Walt Shawman bellowed, quickly coming towards me. He took a quick glance over the side at the Cockney grasping a hanging ladder.

"Did you do that?" Shawman's eyes blazed at me.

I stood back not knowing what to expect either from Shawman or this Cockney clown. "He should not have hit the boy, especially with a rope's end," I said angrily, my eyes on my dripping enemy clambering on board. Buggered, I thought if I was going to back down: not when I was in the right.

"The boy's a lazy little bastard, Mister Shawman," the Cockney spluttered, wiping water off his face. "You should not have him in your crew," he added, gingerly feeling his jaw where I had hit him.

"That was the Captain's decision, Joe, not mine." Shawman bit back.

Now, the girls were there each trying to make sense of the situation.

"West knocked that man overboard for hitting Jacques!" Simon cried excitedly, clearly enjoying what he saw as fun, and me the hero.

I glared daggers at him for making the situation worse, even if it was unintentional. The girls looked at me in a puzzled way, not quite believing Simon, and that someone peely-wally as myself was capable of doing such a thing. Then again, I could not blame them.

"You better get yourself dried off," Shawman ordered Cockney Joe tersely, adding, " Have the cook take a look at that jaw as well."

I turned away, catching sight of Peter talking to Jacques by the stern. The boy had not come to see what it was all about, no doubt he still felt awkward in Jenny's presence.

"You should have kept out of it West." Sarah linked her arm in mine and walked with me to the seats by the mast. "That big brute looked as though he wanted to kill you."

"I must remember not to take any midnight strolls along the deck by myself, especially by the rail."

We sat and Sarah squeezed my hand. "I'm serious, West. Walt Shawman does not seem the kind daddy he appeared to be when he first invited us on board."

Suddenly, I wished we were homeward bound, or better still I could hitch hike on a passing fishing boat or that Flipper was anywhere in sight who might offer me a lift. It could be so easy to find one's self overboard if this ship's captain or his crew decided to let me walk home, for as sure as hell I couldn't swim there.

I felt myself shake, whether Sarah was aware of it or not she made no sign though she still held my hand.

A short time ago, everything on board had been as peaceful and calm as the sea that I was gazing at. Supper time was going to be awkward I thought: Peter not speaking to Jenny; Shawman probably drawing silently on his cigar, and figuring out what best to do next, and whatever it was he decided would undoubtedly be right, for he was a man used to having his own way, of this I was sure. This vessel alone was testament to it.

I closed my eyes in the hope that by doing so it would eradicate what had just taken place, and at first was not aware of the high pitched cry of 'Geronimo' only of Sarah letting go of my hand and jumping to her feet, and instinctively I followed suit, wondering what the heck was going on, when I saw Simon launch himself off the rail into the sea.

"Simon!" Sarah yelled and ran to where the little boy had disappeared.

We both arrived at the same time, each searching the sea below. A little astern, Marco, stood beside Jacques, leaning over the side to see what was happening below, Peter letting out a shriek, and shouting out his brother's name.

Suddenly beneath where Sarah and I stood, Simon emerged. He flipped on to his back and waved a hand to his brother. "Come on in Peter, the water's great!"

"I'll give you great!" Sarah stepped sharply to where a ladder hung over the side. "Come up here this instant, young man." Her voice though angry was tinged with relief.

Peter ran to where the ladder hung, intent on joining his brother. "Coming, Simon."

"No you're not." Sarah stood in his way.

Peter's smile disappeared. "You can't stop me Sarah, I can jump from the rail if I want to. He pointed downwards. "Look, Simon's enjoying it, the sea is calm enough. We will be all right," he pleaded.

"Let the little squirt drown." Jenny joined us. "I mean you Peter, not your brother," her voice was filled with sarcasm.

At first, Peter looked hurt by the remark before his expression changed to one of indecision on whether or not to defy Jenny. Or, should he instead obey her, and perhaps help to reconcile the situation between them?

For a moment, he stood there watching his brother swim towards the bow, then having made up his mind, leaned over the rail, and laughing encouraged him to swim faster.

Simon had reached the bow, he dived and I watched his head then his shoulders disappear. I gave a shudder.

"He'll be all right," Sarah assured me by my side. "But I do wish he'd come aboard now."

"How can he see where he's going under water with his eyes closed?"

Sarah let out a laugh. Jenny heard and joined in. "He will have his eyes open. You can, you know."

I shook my head. "I can't even do that in the shower."

While we spoke, my eyes were on the spot where Simon had dived and there was still no sign of him. I stole a glance at Sarah. Outwardly, she appeared unworried, but I wondered what she was really feeling inside. The boy had not surfaced for what I thought had been a long time, and I was imagining all sorts of things that could be happening to him down there. I looked anxiously around expecting someone to take some action, though as a landlubber, I did not know what. Marco and Jacques still stood together plainly interested in what was taking place; the Captain looking down from the cockpit; Shawman or Cockney Joe or any other of the crew nowhere to be seen.

Anxiously, I looked to where Simon had disappeared when suddenly he resurfaced and swam some distance from the yacht, and I saw him look to where he had dived, clearly something had frightened him, and immediately I thought of all the dangerous and nasty things that could be found in the sea.

"Simon ! Simon!" Jacques was shouting and gesturing at a point a little way off between the swimmer and the hanging ladder where a white fin was gliding through the water.

"Jesus!" Jenny cried and bent over the rail, she too pointing at the white fin. "Simon! Simon! Look! Swim for your life!"

Sarah threw a hand to her mouth, stifling a scream, and gripped my arm, at what was happening below. Suddenly, she let go of my arm and ran towards the ladder and I pulled her back. There was nothing she could do, and worse still she knew it.

"He'll never make it, the shark is between him and the ladder," she sobbed, already seeing the wee boy in the monster's jaws. I too watched in horror, feeling more useless than I had ever felt in my life and wishing with every swear word that I knew that I had never seen this accursed yacht or its owner.

Intently, my eyes alternated between the boy and the fast approaching shark. I heard a splash and saw Marco, a knife gripped between his teeth swim towards the shark, intent on intercepting it before it reached the boy, who, now aware of the danger, was now swimming for his life.

For a moment, the shark disappeared and when it resurfaced held a struggling yelling Marco in its jaws, who continued to stab at the voracious fish with what little strength was left to him. His midriff now almost entirely devoured, the man stabbed and stabbed, each dying blow a defiance. Then, it was all over, the monster, Marco still in its jaws disappeared, and only a blood red circle stained the water where the brave man had fought to save a little boy he scarcely knew.

I stared in horror at what only a few minutes ago had been a peaceful happy scene when I heard another splash, and Jacques was swimming to meet Simon, intent on guiding him away from that red circle of blood.

Some distance away, a fin showed on the surface and I heard a shot ring out, quickly followed by another. I turned to see Captain Valleye, rifle in hand fire volley after volley at the retreating fish until his weapon was empty and he threw it aside in anger and frustration.

Now, Jacques was helping the near hysterical little boy on board, Jenny rushing forward to hug him to her, while Peter wailed his brother's name over and over again.

Sarah left me to help the girl and I held back, as I felt that as these people who had lived and holidayed together might find my presence an imposition. Sad that it was, that it had taken the life of a good brave man to bring them all together again. Simon released himself from Jenny's embrace to say something to Sarah and I was unprepared for what happened next, when out of nowhere, his eyes blazing Walt Shawman pounced upon Simon, and without warning, struck the little boy a fierce blow across the face which sent him screaming to the deck.

"You little son of a bitch you have killed one of my best men," Shawman yelled, and moved to strike Simon again and would have done so had not Jacques thrown himself between his boss and the boy.

I hurried to help. At last, now, there was something I could do, even if it meant that I might be that shark's second course. I cursed again, wishing that my brother Fenton was here.

"No need for that, Mister Shawman." I rounded the man to Jacques side, while Sarah helped the weeping boy to his feet.

"No need for that?" he yelled at me. "He got Marco killed! Had he wanted to go for a swim he should have said. There are snorkels and every other damned thing he could have used had he asked!"

Turning sharply on his heel, Shawman threw over his shoulder angrily. "Keep that little son of a bitch out of my sight, or I swear, should I clap eyes on him again, he will be fish bait."

Beside me Sarah found a beach towel and wrapped it round the near hysterical boy, while Peter put an arm round his brother's shoulder. "Let's get you into something dry," he said, his voice shaking

"I saw him! I saw him, Peter!" Simon shrieked.

"Steady Simon, go with your brother." Sarah motioned that he should follow him.

"But I tell you I saw him!"

"Yes, yes but it wasn't your fault what happened Simon." Peter tried to console his brother, leading him away.

"I think I might see what's on board that I could give the poor kid to calm him down," Jenny suggested. "Hell knows what's going through his mind at what he saw." She shook her head sadly. "He'll always believe what happened to that poor man was his fault."

I looked out over a sea as placid as it had been before the horror had taken place. Jenny was right, Simon had seen a man literally chewed to pieces before his eyes, the result of him wanting to go for a swim. Did he now wish that he had asked permission to have done so? Or alternatively had there been no shark and Simon had swum peacefully about, would Shawman have chastised him so viciously? I gave a shrug. It was all purely academic now.

Chapter 3

I found them all gathered together in our cabin. Jenny had given Simon something to drink, probably with the intention of calming him down, and he sat on the edge of his bunk, clutching the cup with both hands, his towel now replaced by a blanket, Peter having helped him into a pair of shorts and a white T-shirt.

"I saw him," Simon trembled, his eyes wide with horror. "You believe me, don't you West? No one will listen!" he shouted, and the cup fell to the floor as he stood up. "Please West! Listen!"

Here, I thought was a wee boy close to hysteria at what he had seen. And who could blame him? I myself was having trouble blotting out the image of Marco in the shark's jaws and I wondered what would have gone through my own mind, while bearing the pain together with the realisation that I was dying, and there was no escape. I swallowed. But what a way to die.

Simon ran to me, the blanket falling from his shoulders, "I saw him West! The man in the purple suit! He was hanging from a chain where the anchor is!"

For a moment, we all stood there not knowing whether what the boy had said was the effect of what Jennie had put in his drink, or that he was hallucinating as the result of his recent trauma. Whatever the reason, I thought it time to calm the situation, especially the way everyone was looking at Simon.

"This man in the purple suit, was he the same man we all saw when we came on board?" I asked, fighting to remain calm.

Simon nodded. "The fish were biting him!"

I took hold of the boy's shoulders to calm him down, and I saw his expression soften when I added that I believed him, although I appeared to be the only one by the sounds of disbelief from those around.

"That's why I swam away from the boat. I was scared. Besides, he looked horrible and I didn't want to get close to him or those biting fish. See." Simon held up his arm for my inspection. "One bit me."

"It can't be true, West," Sarah's voice was only a whisper. "If it is, what have we got ourselves into?"

Whatever it was, I wished we were not. Now, I understood why the boy had swam away from the yacht, it was to be free of those fish gnawing and chewing at a dead man, and who at that exact time, had not been immediately aware of the shark. That trauma came later, when he again witnessed the death of another man. Only this time, he felt that it was he who was to blame. Now, I understood this wee boy's hysteria. One trauma in one's young life was more than enough. But two in the same day?

How the man in the purple suit had got there could not in any way be construed as an accident by any stretch on the imagination. Or any stretch of Simon's imagination. I now clearly believed the boy.

Simon stood quietly sobbing while I held him.

"Listen, wee man, it was not your fault that Marco was killed, it was the fault of whoever put that man in the suit down there. Do you understand? Yon shark was probably attracted by the smell of blood, and you just happened to be in the way. Do you understand me? You are in no way to blame, Simon."

I saw the girls flash their gratitude at me. Hopefully, Simon would be one less to have nightmares, I, sure as hell would, and I had not been in the water and in any danger.

"What do we do now, West?" Jenny asked forlornly, sitting down on the side of my bed, her hand clasped together between her knees.

"No need to do anything, lady."

Walt Shawman stood in the open doorway. "Seems the little shit has seen something he should not have seen, and I don't mean the shark."

Shawman stepped into the cabin, Cockney Joe a step behind him, the latter's eyes glaring at me, and I thought I detected a look of pleasure in them.

I sat on Simon's bunk and pulled the trembling boy down beside me. His eyes had never left the American, and I felt his fear, also that he should be held responsible for this man's present predicament? And if so, what he would do to him?

"What happens now, Bluebeard?" Sarah stared up at the big man defiantly.

Shawman gave a shrug of his shoulders. "The plan was that you help me get passed the Coastguard. It has in the past. It pays to appear benevolent to the less fortunate,"

"So we were merely pawns. You did not bring us along out of the goodness of your heart?"

"Yip, you've got it in one, gal." Shawman's eyes travelled around the room until finally resting on Peter on the top bunk. "You should have kept that young brother of yours under control, then I would not have to do what I have to do now."

Peter curled a lip. "Or, as your national hero would say, a man's got to do what a man's got to do."

Shawman laughed at the boy's unexpected reply. "I'll pay that one sonny. You have guts all right, that's for sure."

Shawman took his time in extracting a cigar from its case. His intention no doubt, to instil further fear on us, which I might add he was succeeding in doing, at least to me that was, and it did not take a great deal of imagination to know now that his little game was exposed there was no way he could let us go free.

"However, I thought the game was up when you all met outside the girls cabin the night of the storm when we were in the act of…disposing poor Raymond."

So that was why Shawman was still dressed at that time of the morning, it was not because of the storm, rather that he and his crew were dumping Raymond, the man in the purple suit overboard.

Jenny sprang to her feet and advanced upon the man. " You forget that…"

Before the girl could continue, Shawman had struck her across the face. "Shut the F..up," he roared. "And do not open that mouth of yours again until I tell you to. OK?"

"There was no need for that big man." I stood up, one eye on Cockney Joe, and I fully expected that my outburst would initiate orders from the boss to also have my mouth shut. Perhaps even permanently.

If Shawman intended to do so, he was interrupted by Sarah asking. "You can't possibly dispose all of us?"

I wish she had not voiced what was in all of our minds, at least not here in front of the kids. I sat back down and heard Peter moan from his bunk above, and beside me Simon's strangled cry.

Across from me, Jenny held her jaw, tears flooded her eyes and she had a look of incredulity on her face at the realisation of Sarah's question. For a moment, she made to stand up to confront Shawman again, but obviously thinking better of it decided to sit where she was.

Shawman blew cigar smoke in the air and watched it drift upwards. "I think you forget that a lot of strange and inexplicable things happen at sea. For instance that you all went for a little sail in one of the launches but unfortunately were caught in the storm we had last night and it capsized. There were no survivors." He gave an artificial sigh of regret.

"That could be seen as suspicious, not to say irresponsible to let five…all of whom were inexperienced, sail a boat on their own," I asked, albeit hopefully, that it would make this 'big shot' think again.

Shawman drew me a smile that held no warmth but instead sheer pleasure at what he was about to say. "But you *did* have someone of experience with you. He was called Marco. Do you not remember?"

"You beast, Shawman!" Sarah howled at him. Simon screamed and buried his head in my chest.

Beast was an understatement, for what he had just inflicted on an already distraught child.

Shawman showed no sign that what he had said had upset the young boy, but instead drew again on his cigar, his tone tinged with impatience. "Now I will trouble you all for your cell phones, just on the off chance you might succeed in sending a text off to your loved ones. Or even the authorities," he added sarcastically, and Joe laughed from where he stood leaning on the door jamb.

I thought it was time I confirmed what I thought was going on, even should the answers not be to my liking. "I take it that getting past the Coastguard has something to do with your sea faring activities?"

"Sea faring activities," Joe laughed. "That's rich."

"So is your boss." I stared Shawman in the eye. "Your legal business is only a front for your illegal ones. Am I correct?"

"You are correct man. My sea faring activities as you put it are far and away more profitable than the other kind."

"So you're a smuggler?" Sarah drew in a deep breath.

"Drugs, I bet." Peter moaned.

I saw that Shawman was enjoying himself, and why not, he was in command as usual.

His plans may have gone wrong but, by his attitude, they were in no way disastrous to him. He could easily have us all 'committed to the deep' should he have a mind, and somehow I thought he *did have* a mind.

Now firmly in control, Shawman saw no harm in telling, we the condemned, how his plan was supposed to have worked had not the crewman Chatel made a balls of it.

"Tonight a freighter will arrive, that is why we are anchored here, and will convey its precious cargo to us. My plan was that you should all be having a nice nap after your evening meal while this was happening." Shawman made a gesture of apology. "When you all awoke next morning, it would be as nothing toward had ever taken place and we would all be making for home…albeit after a little detour. But that is no concern of yours now."

Satisfied that he had shown himself to be the master planner, and had literally put the fear of death into us, he shifted tack.

"Joe." Shawman indicated that the man collect the phones. "When you have done this, pay Chatel a visit, and remind him in not too gentle a way that it was he who messed things up by having Raymond entangled on the anchor chain." He turned to us. "You see, it is not really my fault that I have to deal with you lot now. Had my crewman not got it wrong, you would all be sitting comfortable at dinner with not a care in the world and thinking how nice a man I am, and looking forward to that little nap you would have felt coming on."

Cockney Joe stepped into the room, and held out his hand for the phone from Simon while I rose and crossed the cabin to get mine from the top drawer of my bedside table, and turned with it in my hand at the same time that Peter hurled his own phone defiantly at the man, who quickly ducked as it flew past his ear.

"Little shit." Joe seethed and was about to retaliate when a sharp order from his boss restrained him and, as he stooped to pick up the fallen instrument from off the floor, Peter landed on top of him, his fists flailing at the man's upper body.

Before I had thought of joining in, Joe had sent the boy flying, his legs and arms hitting the wooden bunks in the tiny space of the cabin to land unceremoniously at the feet of Shawman, amid the screams of the girls attempting to get out of the way.

Grabbing Peter roughly by the collar of his shirt, Shawman hauled him to his feet, and cursing, Joe started towards the boy, a fist raised, determined to regain his dignity.

At last, I could do something, however futile, except Sarah got there first and planted herself firmly between Joe and her charge.

"Enough!" Shawman roared, and pushed Peter away. "Now the phones."

"Ours are in our cabin." Sarah stepped back and sat down on the edge of my bed.

"Go get them Joe," Shawman commanded.

"Could I ask a favour?" Jenny asked meekly, standing up to face Shawman.

"Ask," was Shawman's harsh reply.

"Could we please be allowed to change into something warmer?" She plucked at her blouse. "We could give Joe our mobiles at the same time."

The big boss's eyes narrowed. "If this is some kind of scheme you girls are thinking of hatching, forget it, Joe here will not be so easy on you both as he was with the kid." He motioned to his henchman to make his way to the door. "I'll take the phones Joe, you might need both hands to deal with these two should they have a mind to try something crazy."

Shawman took the phones and smiled at us. "Don't worry, I will not pry into any of your texts."

"I sent one to my dad," Simon, stared defiantly up at the man. "He'll have you in jail for this."

Shawman spluttered a laugh. "Why should he? He still thinks you are having a whale of a time."

"Should that not be shark of a time, Boss?" Joe guffawed.

Shawman joined in. "Ok. Now, you girls, get those damned phones, and pronto."

Now that the girls had left, I took the opportunity to change from my shorts into a pair of trousers. I had just done so when I heard the sound of a commotion from next door. Puzzled, the boys looked at me expecting an explanation. I could not, but Shawman had the answer to my doing anything about it by the pistol that had suddenly appeared in his free hand. His waving it to have me sit down was clear. I did so.

"The gun's real, West." Simon drew in a deep breath.

Peter sat opposite me, and by his expression, he expected me to do something clever or heroic. After all, had I not thrown Cockney Joe overboard?

I heard a scream, my attempt to rise arrested by Simon clutching my arm. "Don't do anything West. Please," he pleaded nervously.

"I should take the kid's advice if I were you Mister Barns," Shawman advised pointing the gun at me.

Jenny was the first to reappear, Sarah, almost thrown into the room by an angry Cockney.

"Bitch did this to me." Joe pointed to where blood seeped from a cut in his forehead. "Hit me with a lampshade she did when I was taking the phone from the other one."

"Makes you feel lightheaded, does it, Joe?" Peter laughed, although his pun did not go down too well with our captors.

"I told you to watch them, didn't I?" Shawman seethed at his henchman.

"Not your day, is it Joe?" I smirked.

"Could be your last Scotty," he threw back angrily.

Both men backed to the door, where Shawman halted. "Sorry it had to end this way but such is life." He shrugged in a way of apology and closed the door, the sound of a bolt sliding into place behind him.

For a moment, we all sat there, and I thought of how things had turned so dramatically in so short a time. Only yesterday, these same boys were living the adventure of their lives, enjoying being part of the crew: a crew who shortly could be party to their death. I clenched my teeth wishing I had never heard or seen Shawman or his accursed Sea Horse.

Simon held my hand, now no longer the happy devilish wee boy I had at first taken him to be.

It was he who first broke the silence. "How will they do it, West? Not like yon man in the purple suit? Not over the side to be eaten by fish!"

Simon was close to breaking point, and I suspected that although Peter had shown an outward courage and still capable of making the odd joke, he was not so far behind. After all, they were two kids who had done no one any harm, and whose lives had revolved around Private schools and first class holidays, and who I suspected had never really mixed with the hoi polloi. Perhaps I was the first, and not a very good advertisement at that. If they still thought I was brave, they should see me when I was facing the weekly bills.

"We cannot just sit here and wait!" Jenny roared. She too had changed, and I felt that she was hiding something, something other than fear.

"You're one to talk. You weren't much help in there against muscle man," Sarah exploded at her friend.

"We could try and break down the door." Peter jumped down from his bunk. "The doors here are not too thick."

"Then what?" Sarah sighed. "Even if they were not to hear the noise we'd make, they do have guns you know."

"Better than being fed to the fish," Peter bit back, his eyes wide with what I could only describe as disappointment at the girl.

"If we could break down the door and I got to David, he might help to save us," Jenny looked expectantly at us.

"Because he loves you Jenny? Is that why? Maybe you're only thinking of saving yourself," Peter's voice was scathing at the girl he had once adored.

"How could you Peter? You know I wouldn't do that. It is just…" she stopped, having thought better of what she was about to say.

"I don't think you can put too much faith in your friend, Jenny," I ventured. "After all, you have only known him a short while and he *is* one of the crew and has been for we don't know how long, and how many trips like this he might have made."

Jenny stamped her foot in anger. "David would not be party to murder, especially not the boys."

"It's no use us fighting over it," Sarah broke in. "If we are going to do something about it, we better start thinking how, and quick."

"I'm for breaking down the door." Peter's voice rose enthusiastically.

"Me too." Simon stood up and, despite the situation, I had to smile at the wee boy's determination.

"Look! Look, West!" Simon pointed to the porthole. "There's a ship coming!"

The boy was right, a light was reflecting off the glass of the porthole.

"We're saved! It could be the Coastguard!" Simon ran excitedly to look out at the approaching vessel, the fear absent for once from his voice at the thought of us all being rescued.

We crammed around the small window and, over Simon's shoulder, I could see that it was not the boat he had hoped for, but what to me looked to be a freighter.

Now at last this was what Shawman had been awaiting for, his supply ship had arrived.

It didn't take long for the rest to realise that the approaching ship was not the Coastguard. This ship was much larger, and was making its way to our port side, which was on the opposite side from our cabin.

"Now's the time to have a go at that door while they're getting their ill gotten gains aboard, as they say," I said light-heartedly, although I was sure they could all hear my heart pounding above their own at this perhaps being our one and only chance of freeing ourselves.

Simon broke away from us and rushed to the door, pulling with all his strength at the handle.

"Pity the door doesn't open out into the passageway." Sarah took a turn at pulling at the stubborn handle.

"Could hitting it with something help?" Peter suggested looking around for some suitably heavy object.

I did not want to dampen anyone's enthusiasm or optimism but I had already resigned myself that however slight the door may be it would hold fast against our efforts, even should we have a lot more time than I calculated we had against the unloading up on deck.

Sarah had said, had the door opened outward we could have pushed and hit it with everything we had, but that it opened inward made it so very much more difficult,

Jenny was the first to give up. "If only I could get to David," she wailed, sitting down dejectedly on Simon's bunk.

"Not David again, Jenny, please." Peter threw her a look of contemp. Evidently, he no longer saw this forlorn figure as the one he had yearned after not so very long ago.

For a moment, we all stood there, five despondent people, all at a loss as to what to do next, until I became aware of four pairs of eyes looking expectantly at me. I shrugged hopelessly.

"I'm only a car salesman," I said in way of an explanation. Lord, I thought, if they were to know I was a Private Investigator; however small, what would they expect of me?

Sarah leaned against the bunk. "Is there no way out?" Her eyes too were on me, only in hers I saw a deeper desperation, but not I gathered for her own life but for the two boys that had been entrusted to her.

"I could get out through the porthole!" Simon exclaimed running to the window. "Then I could get up on to the deck and come back down and open the door," he shouted with excitement. "I could do it West. Honest!" The boy's eyes gleamed. "Let me try?" He swung from me to Sarah. "Please let me do it Sarah."

Sarah levered herself off the bunk. "No Simon," she said softly. "If you fall you'll drown, and there will be no way we can save you."

"Peter, you know I can do it. You have seen me do harder things than this." Simon said in desperation to his brother.

"It might be our only chance, Sarah."

Surprisingly, it was Jenny who was the first to answer. "No Peter, you can't let your little brother try it."

For a moment, both former adversaries looked at one another, and I saw in each of their eyes that what had happened between them was for the moment put aside.

"I think he can do it, Jenny. I really do," Peter endorsed his brother's claim.

I took a look at the porthole. Unlike most I had seen, it was not round but oblong and opened inwards.

Simon stood beside me. "I can get through that West, no bother."

It was the boy's assurance that had me considering what he said. We had nothing to lose, but the kid had and, if anything happened to him, it would take me a long time to get over it, even although I had known him for only a short time, and after what he had experienced he did not deserve to drown. But who was I to deny him his attempt to live?

I looked at the others.

"If we decide on letting Simon do this, we better hurry, they are not going to be busy all night." Sarah jerked her head towards the ceiling in emphasis.

Simon jumped up on to the chair that stood beneath the window, believing that his attempt at getting through there had been ratified by Sarah's last statement. Reaching up he undid the screws that held it closed and pulled it open.

"What now Houdini?" I asked looking up at him standing there.

Simon studied the gap. "I'll go through backwards. Hold my legs until I can grip the edge of the porthole, then I'll lever myself up. With any luck, I should grab something and reach the deck."

"I can do that, Simon." Peter stood across from me ready to take hold of his brother's right leg while I held the other. "You can do it wee man," he added, giving his brother a playful nip of encouragement.

"Thank you for that Peter, that's all I need." Simon replied faking annoyance and, taking hold of the side of the porthole, he levered himself up.

Peter looked first at me to assure himself that I had a firm grip of his brother's leg then up at his disappearing head.

About waist high, the body halted, and then slid back down into the cabin, and we both let go of Simon's legs.

"I knew it was no use," Jenny moaned, looking on despairingly.

Back on the chair, Simon looked at Peter and me. "My T-shirt got snagged. "If I take it off I know I can do it." He winked at Sarah. "Don't worry Sarah, I will have you out of here in no time." Then, minus his shirt, he was out through that narrow space once more until only his brown legs were left dangling.

Sarah looked gravely at me holding the boy's leg. "If anything should happen."

I too was thinking of the consequences of him losing his footing or, failing to hold on to something up there, and plunge into the deep blue sea; and I did mean deep.

Amid my concern I heard the sound of laughter from above. "Holding a party?" I said flippantly to Peter.

"Or finished with their unloading" Jenny suggested sullenly.

I felt rather than saw Simon's leg stiffen while he searched for a foothold on the porthole's rim. At the same time, the door burst open.

"Come! You must come! Alley!" Jacques stood in the doorway, beckoning us to follow him.

We all turned at this unexpected interruption, and hopefully, deliverance.

"I couldn't reach it." Dejected by his failure, Simon reappeared. He saw Jacques and the open door. "Jacques! You've come to get us out!" he said hopefully and slid on to the chair.

"Bring something heavy to wear." Jacques said not over loudly. "It will be cold in the sea. But you must hurry."

All at once, we scattered to pick up what clothing we could find. The boys their hoodie tops the girls already dressed in jeans, their sweaters, and myself a lightweight jerkin I had bought but not quite for this occasion.

We followed Jacques into the passageway where he halted to put a finger to his lips, signalling silence, and we waited while he ran lightly up the short ladder to the deck above.

We all looked at one another, none of us knowing what the boy had in mind, then he was back gesturing to us to come up on deck.

"You must keep your heads down, you can be seen from the bridge. Or should someone come this way."

Crouching, we followed our rescuer until we reached the stern. "The Mademoiselles will go first, then the boys. We will follow." Jacques pointed downwards. "The dinghy, she is there."

Another bout of laughter reminded us that we had very little time left. Jacques left us, and crouched down rounded a hatch towards the bow.

It was then the figure came at us…me mainly as the others except for Peter, who had by this time a leg over the ladder had began his descent to the dinghy.

"Leave the kids. They will be all right, Shawman won't harm them...he…" David got no further as Jacques came up behind him and hit him with a belaying pin.

I mouthed my thanks at Jacques and started after him. Peter stepped down a rung, and looked up at the young Frenchman. "Don't tell Jenny what you've done to lover boy, or she'll throw herself overboard…or you," he chuckled.

Although I was glad to have escaped from the cabin, and now hopefully the yacht, I was quite unhappy at our means of escape.

I lowered myself into the dinghy, which was too close to water level for my liking, and Jacques handed me an oar. "Push us away, Monsieur West."

I didn't need to have served time before the mast to know what he meant.

"Bon. We are on our way. Now, we must row for our lives." Jacques took hold of the other oar and together we started to row away from our so recent jail.

Jenny took my oar from me and began rowing on her side. Eventually, stroke by stroke, we drew away from the vessel, Jacques steering so that the freighter hid us from the yacht, and therefore hopefully out of sight.

It seemed an eternity, and still it appeared that we had scarcely made any headway, both vessels still only a short distance away.

"We must go faster," Jacques puffed and dug his oar deeper into the water. I took over from Jenny, and Peter gave the tiring young Frenchman a spell. Then, it was Sarah and Simon's turn to do their bit. It needed no stretch of the imagination to know that we amateur sailors were not going in a straight line anything but."

"If we keep going like this, we'll be back where we started," Peter gasped.

"More like a boomerang than a dinghy," I added sourly.

"Old people." Simon shook his head in mock dismay.

It took well over an hour before the two vessels, now set against a darkening sky appeared to be some distance away.

"I think we can have a little rest now." Jacques pulled in his oar and gave his back a rub.

I stared at the expanse of sea around us, troubled by how close it was to the rim of our tiny craft. Lord help us I thought should there be a storm.

Sarah saw how scared I was. "We have a repair kit should anything go wrong, West." Her smile reminded me of one a grown-up would give a frightened child to reassure them that all was well with the world. I made a face back at her. Then we both laughed. Mine I must admit a little shakily.

Simon joined in. "And there's a pump should we puncture, too," the boy giggled mischievously.

"Very funny both of you," I retorted in pretence of being annoyed, but secretly pleased that a modicum of humour had returned, especially to Simon.

We started again, each taking a turn at rowing.

"Now that we are free of the boats, where do we go from here?" I asked of Jacques, digging my oar once more into the dark blue water. "We cannot just keep rowing around until someone shouts come in number seven your time is up."

"Good one, West," Peter congratulated me on my humour.

"Don't encourage him for any favour, Peter," Sarah sighed, although I saw her try to hide a smile.

"There is an island that Mister Shawman uses to hide the drugs, it has no people living there, that is why he has chosen it. On occasions, picnickers from the mainland come in their yachts to swim and lie on the beach. This is on the east side of the island, far away from where the drugs are hidden you will understand. We could make for there." Jacques wiped spray from off his brow.

Jenny took an oar from Sarah. "How far away is it, Jacques?"

"Many hours. That is if I can find it." The boy shrugged in the darkness.

"Shawman will expect us to do just that." Sarah leaned back in her seat, grateful for the respite.

"Why the island, Jacques? Why does he not head straight for home?" was my question.

"Mister Shawman is very clever, very cautious. When he meets the Coastguard again on the way home, they sometimes come on board and search. They find nothing."

"Because all the dope is on the island," Peter piped up.

Jacques nodded. "It is hidden there until a motor launch comes to take it into port. The Coastguard do not stop the launch, it is too small to go far out to sea where the freighter would be."

Sarah let out a whistle. "Very cunning is our Mister Shawman."

It was my turn again to row. "Your boss will know by this time that you are not on board. This being the case it will not take him long to figure that you are with us. So I would hazard a guess that he will also make for this island of yours. He has to stop us somehow."

I felt a slight swell of the sea and bit back an oath at water splashing into our little vessel. Perhaps, there would be no need to search for this island after all.

The slight rocking of our boat did not seem to worry any of the crew, in fact it had the opposite effect on the boys who whooped with glee as we did what to me was a roller coaster.

Chapter 4

I guessed it to be close on midnight when we had finally stopped rowing. I peered at my watch: it was now 3am so I must have dozed off. Across from me, Peter cradled Simon into him, and the girls sat with their heads on their chest, now completely exhausted by their efforts. They, like myself, were not used to using muscles in this way, or in fact in any other way connected with the sea. This we had left to our little shipmates.

I had not liked Jacques' forecast of the island being several hours away. I looked across the vast expanse of water, now gray in the dark of night, trying not to think what lay beneath its surface. Give me terra firma every time. I thought of home. North Berwick had sea too, but give me North Berwick Law every time. At least, there you knew what monsters were below you and I didn't mean VAT men either. I sighed. All this I had done for the pretty face sitting across from me. Would I never learn? I sincerely hoped I would live long enough to find out.

Jacques was the first to start rowing again and, being his partner, so to speak, I too started.

A little later, Sarah sat up with a jolt, her unfocused eyes trying to determine where she was. She looked at me, saw what I was doing and, still half asleep, took hold of her oar and began rowing.

"Not much of a sleep," I said, pulling on my oar.

Sarah yawned, but said nothing, she was not quite ready for small talk so early in the morning.

I turned to the boy beside me. "When…if we reach this island what then, Jacques?"

It took a little time before he spoke. "First, Mister Shawman will look for us on the sea, then when he cannot find us, he will head for the island. He must unload the drugs for the launch, you will understand. He has a timetable, a …

"Schedule," I suggested.

Jacques nodded. "As you say a schedule. It is now Friday, the launch will come tomorrow Saturday. They do not come exactly after the drop has been made, this is to give the freighter some… how do you say…leeway?"

I nodded. "Leeway is right."

Jacques went on. "The launch will not know of the delay, or of Mister Shawman searching for us. It is a rule that there will be no communication between the launch and the yacht, not even in emergencies. The place where they hide the drugs is on the west side of the island. I think Mister Shawman will anchor Sea Horse near the beaches on the east side so that he can watch for any vessel coming to picnic or spend the day there."

"I bet I know why." Now awake, but still sleepy Jenny leaned wearily on her oar. "It's because he will expect us to try and reach any of the so called picnickers. It is our only way off the island. That's if we find the damned place," she added bitterly.

The dawn was still time away and we had not sighted the island. Now and again, I saw the others give Jacques a look which seemed to ask if he did indeed know which way we were headed? Again, we halted for a rest.

"I have to pee." Simon stated prosaically.

. "Me too," Peter joined in.

Now this was going to be embarrassing.

"All right for you guys, but what about us girls? Not so easy for us." Jenny gave each of us a look, expecting an answer, and the right one at that.

"West?" Sarah cocked her head to the side in expectation of my providing a solution.

I had one. Although it required having us all shift positions and probably rocking the boat in the process, which was last thing I had in mind. "I think you should try holding it in unless you are fair bursting." I suggested deadpan.

My little joke was not appreciated.

"Old folk," Simon gave his usual sigh of bewilderment, although I did not think he took what I had suggested too seriously.

"Ok. You boys can turn round from where you are sitting and aim overboard. Then it will be my turn and Jacques's to do the same here."

"We promise not to look," Sarah tittered.

"She won't see mine in the dark from where she's sitting," Simon said positively.

"I won't see yours either Simon, and I will be standing next to you." Peter gave his brother a playful nudge.

"Ok. So what do we do now?" Jenny inquired, and even she had to smile.

"You girls can go first, then Jacques and I will swap places with you two. All us boys will look the other way. Won't we boys?" I warned them.

"On no we won't." Simon called out, mischievously.

"Oh yes you will," both girls echoed together, equally as loud. And we found ourselves all laughing at this unexpected form of pantomime, all except poor Jacques who had no way of understanding this British comedy tradition. And who could blame him?

It worked. At least, at first, when the girls swapped places with Jacques and myself. It was when the girls returned to their places and the boys stood up to take their turn at the side, that the wave hit the dinghy and Simon lost his balance and was over the side before any of us realised it, we ourselves having been too pre-occupied in fighting to retain our balance.

"Simon!" Peter's terrified screech filled the small craft and, throwing off his hooded top, he was over the side before any of us knew what was happening.

Jacques pushed me roughly aside and threw himself down by the rim of the dinghy to peer over the side for any glimpse of the two boys.

"Oh no!" Jenny shrieked. "This cannot be happening."

Sarah and I joined Jacques on peering over the side into that dark ominous water. All my fear of the sea realised. Please God, I thought, not both boys, please not even one. My eyes like organ stops, I scanned all around that dark water, while the girls shouted out hysterically the boys names. Jacques stood up and throwing off his heavy fisherman's jersey balanced himself ready to dive overboard.

I saw, or thought I saw, a darker shape than that of the sea a little distance away, silhouetted for a moment against the skyline. Again I saw it, this time double, or so I hoped. Then Jacques was over the side, for I believed that he too had witnessed what I had seen. I saw him reach the spot, or what I thought was the spot, but now there was nothing. I swallowed hard. And, all the while the girls continued to shout out the boys' names, each cry more desperate than the last, each cry now more a hysterical shriek.

Our small craft seemed to be drifting away from where I had last seen the shapes, with Jacques swimming and resurfacing to gulp in a lungful of air and dive again. The feeling of helplessness hit me again, and I cursed everything that was nautical in the world. The young Frenchman surfaced again, and this time swam further away, and I felt drained by his action which could only mean the shapes I had seen had not been that of the boys.

I peered harder, all the while wondering what Sarah and Jenny would tell the boys' parents at having both their sons lost in this way.

"Sarah! Jenny!" I was sure it was Simon's voice that I heard. It came again, this time too, calling out my name.

I searched around from where the cry might have come from and, seeing nothing, crawled to the other side of the craft and peered into the night, sweeping the short distance from where I thought the sound might have come from.

"Do you see anything?" Sarah asked in desperation by my side, she too scanning the water immediately in front of us.

"Nothing here either!" Jenny cried from the other end of the dinghy, her voice little less than a shriek.

A head appeared some way to my right, and quite close to where Jenny was. Then, I saw an arm, and another head and upper body and Jacques holding Simon.

Jenny leaned over the side to help grab Simon and, with Jacques still in the water, they got the boy on to the rim of the boat, and I helped haul him aboard and lay him on the bottom of the dinghy.

I looked from Sarah to Jenny. "Is he going to be all right?" I looked down at the pale face.

"Help me get these wet tops off him and we'll see," Jenny answered already beginning to strip off the sodden garments. This done she began to work some life into the inert figure.

After what seemed an eternity the boy gave a splutter and vomited up half the ocean.

Sarah gave a little whoop of relief. "I think, thanks to you, Jenny, he will be all right now."

"I hope so," Jenny's eyes were on the wee boy who lay there staring up at her, not quite knowing where he was or what had happened to him.

Jacques had not come aboard but continued to swim around, now searching for Simon's brother.

Now that Jenny did not need any help at present, Sarah caught my eye, the same thoughts coursing through our minds. We had lost Peter.

Another wave hit our craft and I was flung against one of the seats. Water splashed into the dinghy, and I though how ironical it would be to have Simon saved only to be drowned now. I cursed again. Sarah put out a hand to help me rise to my knees, and I made to grab the lip of the craft when I felt another hand there, one which was wet and cold. Then, another hand appeared and I heard Sarah cry out, "Peter!"

Now on my knees I grabbed at the hands and began to pull until Peter's face appeared. I let out a yell of unembarrassed jubilation at this unexpected sight and pulled harder. "Where the hell have you been?" I shouted down at him, pulling him on board.

Peter lay for a moment, recovering his breath and then through a cough stared up at me. "Well I needed to pee, didn't I?"

Sarah and I laughed, as much with relief at the boy being alive as his quip.

I could have hugged him but thought better of it. After all, what would people think? Fortunately, Sarah was not so restrictive, she bent down and gave Peter a peck, or might I say a little more than a peck on the cheek.

"That's enough," I said in mock annoyance, "Sarah is supposed to be my date for tonight," I dared not say that she was my girl just in case I found myself over the side.

"Where's Simon? Is he safe?" Peter struggled to rise. "I saw Jacques swim to him."

"Your brother's safe, Peter," Sarah assured him. I concurred and helped to get him on to a seat, away from the wet floor of the dinghy.

Peter looked to where, with Jenny's help his brother had managed to sit up. "Some pee eh Simon?" he grinned weekly.

"I don't need one now Peter," Simon said solemnly.

Sarah helped Peter out of his wet top, and taking a handkerchief from her pocket did her best to dry his shivering body in the cold night air and no doubt also the after affects of his recent experience.

For my part, I took off my jerkin and tossed it to him. "Here, that should help a wee bit." I pointed a finger at him in mock warning. "But don't get it wet. OK?"

"OK West."

Jenny threw Peter his dry hooded top which he had pulled off before diving in to save his brother. "Thanks Jenny." He gave her a shaky smile. After what he, and all of us, had gone through it was no time to hold grudges.

Huddled against Jenny, Simon called out hoarsely, "Thanks for saving me Jacques. I'll tell Mum and Dad what you did."

Jacques made a sign that he had heard and appreciated the thanks.

"How you found him I'll never know, Jacques, but you did save his life," I said, helping to pull his dry heavy jersey over his head. "Good thing you took this off before you went for that swim of yours, I only have the one jerkin."

The boy nodded and gave a shiver. "I did not think that I would find the little boy, Monsieur West," he said, softly, not wanting the boy to hear. "It was only because I saw his hand in the air thrashing about that I found him. He had swallowed much water and could not cry out, you understand. But I could not find Peter anywhere. I thought he was gone."

A little later, I sat there, the only one I believed to be awake. I looked to the rear of our craft where Simon sat fast asleep huddled against Jenny, then to the middle, where Peter and Sarah sat dozing, their heads dropped upon their chests and, beside me, Jacques, now completely exhausted, leaned on my shoulder in a well earned rest.

Now almost asleep myself, and satisfied that there were no icebergs in the vicinity, I, as was our dinghy, content to drift off, at least for a little while.

I was the first to come awake, after a troubled night's sleep, still unable come to terms with how small and, to me, fragile our little vessel was in this large deep scary ocean. Several times, I was sure I had seen a fin and choked with the thought of those large sea monsters capsizing our small craft and having us for a midnight take- away. I was glad that at least Simon was fast asleep, and not sharing my fear of believing to have sighted a shark or two, and shuddering at the thought of how much more the wee lad could take. But fear can last only so long before tiredness or resignation cuts in and, therefore I must again have fallen asleep, for we all seemed to come awake almost at the same time.

Jacques mumbled an apology at having used my shoulder as a pillow. Peter sitting beside Sarah sat up and yawned across from me with Sarah joining in, while Jenny stared around her mystified at finding herself there and not quite knowing why, and Simon for his part edging away from the girl's protective shoulder, and flexing his muscles amidst a yawn, and I fully expected him to shout Tarzan in the process.

By midday, the heat from the Mediterrian sun was at its fiercest and, with the exception of the girls, we all sat bare topped. The three boys a deep shade of brown, while I sat like a stalk of celery courtesy of North Berwick's global warming.

I ran my dry tongue over even drier lips. Our becoming that bit more irritable with one another was a measure of how thirsty we all were, and I wondered how long we could go on before we gave up rowing completely.

We had all assumed our original rowing positions, with Jacques and myself at the front, the girls on the middle seats and the boys at the rear, when Simon let out a sigh similar to someone who had missed out on winning a jackpot by one number. "I'm hungry, is there anything to eat or drink?"

Without altering her paddle stroke, or turning her head, Jenny answered with an unequivocal, "No. What do you think this is, a cruise ship?"

"This dinghy was not meant to be used for emergencies," Jacques explained. "It does not carry food or water. It is used mainly when anchored off shore."

"How long do you think we can last without water, or something to eat?" Peter asked me.

I gave a shrug. "I haven't a clue in these matters Peter. Do you Jacques?"

"Sometimes three days without water, but not in this heat."

"Are we anywhere near this island of yours?" Jenny sounded desperate.

While the young man took his time to answer, I studied the girl who sat running her fingers through her hair in exasperation. When first we met, I would have taken her to be the stronger willed of the two women, but here she was close to breaking point. Yet, only last night, she had been instrumental in reviving Simon, showing nothing other than resilience, and remaining reasonably calm when searching for Peter. Plainly something was troubling her, though I did not know what. Was it being parted from David? But, according to Sarah, she had only known the man a week prior to our little sail.

Was her love for him so deep in so short a time? I gave a little sigh. Nothing was impossible where love was concerned. As my old uncle used to say, love is an itch you cannie scratch laddie. Maybe in this case he was right.

While these thoughts coursed through my mind, Jacques held up a hand to shade his eyes from the sun, and I put my shirt on as my back began to nip. "I think the island will lie somewhere over there," he answered, pointing.

"I hope so," Peter sighed. "I think we are going round in circles. I'm sure that we've past that same wave before."

The boy's unexpected quip had us all laughing and, for a moment, we forgot our troubles.

At Jacques instruction, we set too with what little will we had left, rowing in the direction he thought the elusive island might lie. After an hour or more, there was still nothing around us but deep blue water.

Again, we had to halt for a rest. Each rest had become more frequent and, in turn, we rowed less.

Simon sat with his back against the rubber side of the boat. Even with his suntan, he looked pale. How much could the kid take I thought? How much could any of us take? Then it came to me that I had been so involved in my concern for the boy that I had forgotten about his brother. Peter was only a couple of years or so older, and still a boy, who had also gone through a lot. Now he too sat back beside his brother, his legs stretched out before him as far as they would allow in this cramped space.

Simon saw me looking at him, and I gave him a wink of reassurance. He tried to smile, but the effort seemed to be too much for him, and he closed his eyes that by doing so when he opened them again it would all have been a bad dream.

"Look!" Jacques gave me a nudge. "There! Over there! Is that a ship?"

His cry had us all following his pointing finger. Sarah squeezed my hand, and the look she gave me told it all. Should this ship be the Sea Horse, then Shawman would have an easy job of finishing what he had intended to do after his scheme had been discovered. The only difference was that it now included Jacques.

Simon had recovered sufficiently to stand up and wave his arms excitedly at the distant vessel. Besides Sarah and myself, I did not know what were the thoughts of the others.

The dilemma was, that we would all be happy to see the vessel steer in our direction, should it not be the Sea Horse, but if was, we were all as good as dead. Again to see the vessel disappear into the distance and it was not Shawman's yacht, what then?

Jacques stood up, his hand over his eyes peering intently over that vast expanse of blue water, during which time the distant vessel had neither grown or diminished in size.

Suddenly, Jenny grabbed an oar. "What are we all waiting for? We should be rowing! If we can get closer they might see us."

"And, if it is the Sea Horse, Jenny, what then?" Peter asked. This time, I was relieved that he had made no comment about her wanting to see her David again.

"Anything would be better than starving or thirsting to death in this." She threw her oar down, angrily.

"I don't think we need worry, the ship *is* a yacht, but not Sea Horse." Jacques confirmed his deductions by sitting back down.

"Have they seen us?" Simon asked excitedly all weariness having left him for the moment.

"I don't think so, Simon," Peter said despondently. "In fact, I should say they are going further away."

It was true, for it was now plainly visible to each of us that the ship was sailing out of sight.

Dejectedly, we all sat down, heads bent, studying the bottom of our boat, all alone with our thoughts, and I believed all our thoughts were the same: that all hope was lost.

It took a while after the ship's disappearance to find the inspiration necessary to begin rowing again. Despite the occasional slight breeze, the heat was oppressive, and I was forced to discard my sweat sodden shirt once more.

Peter stood up to pull away the seat of his shorts that were clinging to him. "I think my shorts are riveted to my backside, West," he apologised, giving them another tug.

"I hate to think what mine are like, but I think I could win the sticky bum contest," I answered, tugging at my own.

Sarah laughed across at me. "And don't ask us girls either."

Jenny's head came up. "That goes for me too, Peter," she said, without turning round to face him.

"I'll take your word for it Jenny," the boy answered, his eyes on the girl's back. And I heard a little warmth there.

It was early evening, just when I thought that we would have to spend another miserable night at sea that Peter let out an excited cry. "Is that land over there, or is it just clouds?" He pointed his oar in that direction.

"It *is* land!" Jenny shouted from where she sat in front of the boy. "I'm sure it is!" This time there was desperation in her voice.

"I think you may be right." Jacques dropped to his knees, his hands on the side of the boat, his eyes glued to where he thought the island might be.

I peered over his shoulder. "If they are clouds we are seeing, they certainly haven't moved since we first sighted them.

"Let's go for it," Peter called out. "We have nothing to lose."

Better than chasing rainbows, I thought. But should it turn out to be clouds we would have used up most of our energy in a useless chase which in turn could be taking us away, instead of closer to our elusive island.

However, we all set too with a will, each doing their bit then handing their oar to their partner to take over when it was their turn.

A little later, Peter called across excitedly to me, "It is land, West!"

I shared the boy's enthusiasm. Now that we were closer I could make out the rugged outline of an island and I hoped it was the one we had been searching for. Then again, if it was not, did it really matter? At least we would be on dry land.

We were all so intent on staring across the deep blue water that at first we were unaware of the reason for the bump on the side of our boat, until I saw the outline of a fin, then another, and I almost lost all control of my bladder.

No, not now, not when we were so close to safety, I whispered shakily.

Another bump. This time everyone saw the sharks swimming past. Simon let out a low frightened sob, and grabbed his brother's arm.

Watching the sharks draw closer, Sarah managed through her fear to say my name.

Resigned to her fate, Jenny just sat there, rocking back in forth repeating over and over again, "This was not supposed to have happened when I took the job. God help us."

Beside me, Jacques threw me a look that asked if I knew what to do. I threw him back a look that said I didn't.

Again, the boat was rocked by our hostile foe and I imagined myself in the water my legs dangling awaiting the excruciating pain of one of those massive jaws tearing into my leg. Was I about to find out what poor Marco had experienced?

This time, one voracious fish drew closer than the others, and I stood up and hit it as hard as I could with the blade of my oar. It seemed to do the trick, not for the shark but for me, now anger replaced my fear and I hit one of its pals when it too drew near. Then, we were all hitting and stabbing for our lives, the boat rocking and swaying, the result of our combined efforts.

"Get that one, Peter!" Simon pointed, calling out excitedly to his brother, while Jacques warded off another one from where he and I were crouched over the side of the boat.

One came closer, and I saw the row of enormous jagged teeth. It butted our boat and, for one terrifying second, I thought it had succeeded in capsizing us into the middle of its pals. Then, amazingly, our small craft righted itself throwing me in the direction of our menace and I struck out at it with all my strength before the craft had me stumbling backwards.

Jacques stood above me and hit my shark, and this time it turned away.

"Did you see those teeth, Monsieur West?" he gasped in disbelief.

Still recovering from my close encounter of the voracious kind, I replied weakly, "And not a filling amongst them."

Jacques gave me a quizzical look then burst out laughing, Sarah too and, still laughing related my joke to the others, it appearing that our seagoing enemies had had enough, having disappeared as quickly as they had appeared.

His chest heaving with excitement Simon stared at me. "They've gone West. Haven't they?"

I took a last quick look around. "Seems so, Simon. We beat them off. Now they know whose boss. Ok." I sounded more confident than I felt, for I was still inwardly shaking, but I knew that I must give the wee boy some reassurance.

"I clouted one as it swam past," Peter informed us excitedly, examining his oar for any tell tails marks, or, I suspected dents to his weapon.

Exhausted, we all sat down.

"Do you think they have really all gone?" Sarah's body seemed to shrink as she asked the question.

I nodded. "I think there will be a few looking for a couple of aspirins after the way we went about hitting their craniums, I should say." I sought to sound reassuring, and gave a little chuckle.

"Or a couple of band aids," Peter laughed, adding to my joke.

It took less than an hour before we were running close to the shoreline of our island. Jacques pointed to a rock jutting out into the sea. "It is the correct island, West. On the other side of that big rock is where we unload our cargo."

"You are sure of this, Jacques?" Sarah asked the boy.

"Oui, Sarah. I have been here three times before."

"Do you think Sea Horse has been here, Jacques?" Then, I thought how stupid a question it was. The yacht was not likely to have left signs such as car tracks, or anything.

Jaqcues shook his head. "The only way to find out is to take a look where the drugs are stored."

I snapped a look at my watch, and my limited experience of the area told me it would be dark in an hour or so. "You think that the motor launch will be here tomorrow?"

This time, Jacques gave a shrug. "If things had gone according to plan for Mister Shawman, I think yes. But, as I said before, the launch might leave it until Sunday, if they do not see Sea Horse coming back into port tomorrow. But we must hope it will come tomorrow."

"Suppose we were to find somewhere to hide tonight, but no so far away that we could go back to this hideout of theirs and wait for the launch to arrive tomorrow…hopefully."

"You have a plan West?" Sarah asked resting from rowing.

"A bit of one." I turned back to Jacques. "How many men will come with the launch do you think?"

"Usually two or three, it depends on the size of the cargo." I nodded. Jacques went on. "If we row a little further up the coast, the ground is higher and, from there, you can see to the other side of the island. At least to where I think Sea Horse will be anchored so that should we land on that side of the island they can see us arrive, and if so stop us from making any contact with any others who would also be anchored on that side."

"You mean picnickers?" Sarah asked.

"Can we go ashore now, West? I'm starving," Simon pleaded.

"We are going to row a little bit further, until we can find a place to land," Jenny answered.

We had gone about half a mile beyond the rock Jacques had first recognised, when we saw a smooth stretch of beach.

"This will do, West. We will row ashore here."

Jacques decision suited all of us and we started to put our backs into rowing. A wave higher than the rest obliged by tossing us onto the sandy beach and we all scrambled out of our little craft as if it was sinking.

Solid earth, or in this case sand, had never felt so good and safe under my feet.

In an instant the boys were off intent on finding water while the rest of us hauled our small home ashore and hid it in the undergrowth. This done we sat, or lay, on the beach, exhausted.

In no time it seemed the boys were back calling out excitedly that they had found a small stream and, although relieved, we wearily got to our feet and followed them. Never had water tasted so good and ashamedly I drank until my aching stomach could hold no more.

The boys in contrast no sooner had their fill than they were off exploring their new surroundings and once again I had to marvel at their resilience, while now that my thirst had been slated…at least for the time being all I wanted to do was lean my back against a tree and fall asleep.

"I hope they don't go too far and get lost." Sarah sounded worried.

"They'll be all right," Jenny assured her companion. "Just think what they've been through."

I had to admit she was right. If they had survived shark attacks and human ones, then these woods should not hold too much of a threat.

"Once they have seen enough, they will be back…hungry too." Sarah searched each of our faces. "Then what do we do?"

"Food for thought?" I should say, I curled a lip, although I knew what she meant. It was not only the boys who were hungry, and I found myself calculating the last time we had all eaten which had been yesterday afternoon, Mister Shawman having denied us an evening meal after our discovery of his plans.

"It will not be too long until it is dark," Jacques moved away from the dinghy. "There is a hill not so very far away, which, if I can reach, I will be able to see part of the other coast. If Sea Horse is there, and anchored where I think she will be, then I can come back and tell you. Then we can make a plan. Oui?"

"What plan would that be?" Jenny looked directly at me.

"Hopefully to relieve some would be smugglers of their small vessel." I made a face in the way of a smile.

"You mean steal the launch when it arrives tomorrow...*if* it arrives tomorrow and we have not all died of starvation." Jenny's look was one of disbelief.

"Have you a better plan?" Sarah challenged her.

Jenny nodded. "Give ourselves up. I'm sure Mister Shawman would not kill all of us, especially the boys."

"He said he would before. I mean all of you. Should any of you escape it would put an end to all his plans, all his schemes, all his empire, besides having to go to jail." Jacques concluded his little speech with a Gallic type of gesture. "Now I must go before it is too late. Oui?"

I was happy at what the boy had said, not only did it make sense but it effectively terminated a conversation I was reluctant to continue, especially about my forthcoming plan which as yet was neither fourth coming or even fifth coming.

We heard the boys chattering excitedly before we saw them. Simon came to me and held up a handful of berries for examination and hopefully also my approval. "Can we eat these West?" he asked eagerly.

"Where did you find them Simon?" Jenny furrowed her brows dubiously.

"Not in the supermarket I can assure you," was my conclusion. "No sell by date either," I added, handling one suspiciously.

Peter offered one to Sarah. "Do you think we can eat them?"

"So you want a second opinion?" I quizzed the boy.

"Yes, doctor."

"Can we eat them or not?" Simon cried out in exasperation, lifting his eyes to the heavens.

"Well if you do, you should know by tomorrow at the latest whether you should have or not. It's up to you."

"Some doctor," Peter tut-tutted.

I looked at the girls for help. Both gave a nonchalant shrug, and left the decision to me.

"I'll try one," Simon decided, putting one in his mouth.

"Where's Jacques?" Peter asked, while his brother cautiously chewed.

"He's gone to find out if Sea Horse is on the other side of the island," I explained. Peter acknowledged my explanation with a nod.

We all stood watching while Simon chewed delicately, his expression changing from one of acceptance to doubt, then resignation before swallowing with a gulp.

"Not bad." He popped in another one and chewed much more convincingly.

Also convinced, we all gave one a try. I halted at four. After all everything, or almost everything, depended on me tomorrow. And should things go wrong and I had to run, I wouldn't need the undesired effects of these berries to help me do so.

An hour later, it was completely dark and the boys had at long last exhausted themselves and their tale of what they had seen in the woods, which was nothing other than what we had witness ourselves.

Our feast over, the boys complete with hooded tops lay curled up next to one another in our small home, Jenny at the other end.

"Where are you and Sarah going to sleep?" Simon yawned at me.

Peter gave his brother a dig in the ribs. "Don't ask silly questions, stupid."

Sarah gave me a look of embarrassment. "We're going to meet Jacques on his way back." It was not a complete lie, or was it?

"See you in the morning, you two. Please don't make a noise should you decide to come aboard in the wee small hours." Jenny threw each of us a knowing look.

It was the first time that I had Sarah to myself. We walked in the direction Jacques had taken and, whether it was tiredness or shyness that had us remain silent, I do not know, until we came to the spot where we had come ashore, and taking my hand Sarah led me to the beach.

"We could miss Jacques if we go much further," I said hoarsely.

"You haven't gone very far yourself, West Barns. Do I have to give you instructions?"

Suddenly, the night was filled with stars, violins played in the background, mermaids sang off shore, and my four berries, started to make a return journey. I hoped they tasted better second time around as Sarah was about to find out as she kissed me passionately on the mouth.

When she had done, and there was no visible side affects I attempted to taste *her* berries. First kiss, I was not too convinced, so I tried again. Next time, the berries tasted better when we lay on the sand.

"Now, are you glad you came on the cruise?" Sarah lay on her side a hand propping her head.

I nodded. "I didn't like the part about the sharks though. Or of the boys going overboard. Lucky for Simon, Jenny knows first aid."

"Oh I can do that too," Sarah said, not to be out done.

"Mouth to mouth?"

She nodded. "Want a demo?"

"Only if it's on NHS, I can't afford Bupa."

She tried anyway.

All too soon, it was time to head back and, just for a short while, we had succeeded in forgetting our dilemma. Now we had to face it again.

Even while a little away from our orange dinghy we saw that Jacques had not returned. I halted. I had to think, and what I was thinking was no credit to the young man who had helped save our lives.

Sarah squeezed my hand. "What's up, doc? Is it the berries?" she chuckled.

I shook my head. "The hill that Jacques intended reaching to see if Shawman's yacht was anchored in the bay, or where ever he thought it might be, is not so very far away."

"And?" Sarah stared up into my troubled eyes.

"He said he wanted to reach it before dark, so I would have thought that he would have been back by now."

"Do you think something might have happened to him, West? Is that it?"

So many things were going through my mind. Perhaps, he had lost his way coming back and had decided to bed down for the night where he was. Or he had gone further than the hill, not having seen the yacht from where he had expected. Or that the yacht was not there at all but further up the coast, which would be as good a reason as any for him not having returned in the dark.

Slowly, I conveyed my deductions to Sarah, who stood silent for a moment or so, before saying softly, "But that's not what's worrying you? Is it West? I nodded. "You think he might have gone back to Shawman? But surely not. Not after what he has done for us. Remember, it was he who came to our rescue, by providing the dinghy."

"I know, Sarah." I leaned my back against a tree. "Except, he might have thought it over and decided we didn't stand a chance of getting off this island so instead has tried to ingratiate himself with his boss on the off chance that by telling him our whereabouts he might be forgiven his earlier transgressions…or words to that affect."

"If he has, we are sunk," Sarah shuddered.

"We move first thing tomorrow. If Jacques has betrayed us, he is certain to lead his cronies straight here."

"Somehow I don't think I will get much sleep tonight." Sarah shuddered again.

I levered myself off the tree. "And if things had been different, you would not have gotten much sleep either." I made a face and gave her another wee kiss.

Chapter 5

Similar to Sarah, I didn't get much sleep either. In fact, I didn't sleep well at all. Even as the first light of dawn shone on the huge golden ball rising from the sea, I had awoken Sarah, who in turn, aroused Jenny while I gave the boys a shake.

"We have to move." I did not want to further shatter their hopes by disclosing my suspicions of Jacques having betrayed us and, with it, any chance of our stealing the launch when it came. "We will move closer inland on the off chance that Shawman knows we are on the island. First, we hide the dinghy."

Peter cut me short. "Where's Jacques?" he scanned around him in expectation of seeing the young Frenchman.

"He should be back shortly, Peter." Sarah saved me the trouble of explaining.

A little later, while busily trying to hide our dinghy, a sudden rustle in the undergrowth, brought us all to an abrupt halt. Had we been found? I cursed and searched around for any type of weapon, suitable or otherwise.

"Monsieur West!"

I had never been so glad to hear a French voice.

Jacques greeted us all with a wave of his hand and a grin from ear to ear.

"I thought you had got lost." There was no denying the relief in Sarah's voice.

"Me too," I added.

Jacques shook his head. "No. I saw Sea Horse from the hill. She was where I thought she would be. She lies off shore towards the foot of the island. It is a good place to see any ship arrive from there. Also, they would see us if we were to attempt to contact any visitors to the island."

"What's that you've got on your shoulder Jacques?" Simon interrupted, pointing excitedly.

In turn, the young Frenchman threw me a look. "It is something I brought from Sea Horse." He slipped the backpack from off his shoulders, and we all looked on in eager anticipation while he opened it.

"I could only bring a few apples, oranges and three bananas, you understand, nothing heavy or which had to be cooked. And a box of matches just in case."

"You beauty!" Jenny stepped forward and gave him a kiss on the cheek.

"Merci, mademoiselle." Jacques grinned his pleasure. "I also managed to rescue this from the galley. It was not easy. Ta ra!" he sang, pulling a chicken out of the bag in a way a conjurer would, and posing, held it up for our inspection with a "Voila!"

Our removal to the beach temporary delayed, we all sat around munching the chicken.

Sarah tore off a piece and handed it to Jacques. "Here, Jacques, you are entitled to the most. You have worked hard enough for it, not to mention the danger you put yourself in."

We all munched our agreement.

"Should we keep some for later?" Jenny looked around for a consensus of opinion.

"Don't think so, Jenny," Simon answered seriously. "In this heat, it could go off."

"Not much chance of that, Charlie Horse," I made a face at him.

"I think little Simon is correct in what he says," Jacques added his support to the boy's deductions.

"Ok. Let's finish it." Jenny gave in graciously, but I also noted gratefully. "But we will keep the fruit." Narrowing her eyes, she peered at Simon in mock severity, "Fruit can last a bit longer you know, little boy."

It was surprising what a little food could do to raise moral, Jenny for one seemed to be more at ease, happy even. The boys chattered away to one another in a way that suggested nothing untoward had ever happened, and I admired their resilience.

Jenny was put in charge of what was left of the provisions Jacques had managed to acquire from the yacht, which she said, with a pretended hostile glare at Simon, she would guard with her life. He, in return, pulled a wee boy's comical face.

"Do you still intend attempting to take the launch when it comes, Monsieur West?" Jacques sat chewing the last of his chicken.

"I don't know, Jacques," I answered dubiously. "Now that you have stolen food from the yacht they now know we are here and, if I were Shawman, I would surmise that the only alternative we have of getting off this island is either courtesy of some passing ship, or trying to get hold of the launch when it arrives."

The boy nodded his understanding. "Perhaps I have done wrong, Monsieur West."

"No Jacques, you did the right thing." I assured him. "How long do you think we could have lasted without your food?

"Are we going to take over the launch when it comes, West?" Simon asked eagerly.

I was unsure what the boy meant by 'we' but I hazarded a guess at what he meant.

I turned my attention back to Jacques. "How do you think Shawman will come? By launch from his yacht? Or will he come overland by the same route you took to get back here?"

Jacques's answer was precise and to the point. "He will not use his own launch for fear that you would see it, even if he were to leave it some distance from here and journey the rest on foot."

"Pity," I drew a deep breath. "Were he to have done so, we might have had a crack at going for it, instead of the one we hope will arrive today. With any luck, Shawman might have left this one unguarded. But your answer has put paid to this." I thought for a moment. "How many men can Shawman rely on?"

It was the French boy's turn to ponder, before he finally said," Mister Shawman will not come himself, neither will the captain. These will remain on board. I should say Cockney Joe, as you call him, Steve the cook, Chatel who I don't think you have met, at least not spoken to, Chatel, he is the one who made a bottom of drowning Raymond," he explained, and we all chuckled at his description, "And, of course, David."

At this last name, Jenny gave a gasp of horror, and I quickly silenced any comment that Peter was likely to make with an evil glare. It did the trick and I continued with my deductions. "That makes four at least, not counting those who will arrive by launch."

Sitting on the grass, while I pondered, Peter asked of Jacques, "Did you have to swim out to the Sea Horse? Or was it anchored near the shore, Jacques?"

"Not too far out Peter, but it was more difficult swimming back with the pack on my back."

"I'll bet." Simon's eyes shone in admiration.

"I don't know how you didn't get caught when you went about getting all those things for us?" Sarah shook her head in disbelief.

"I was very quiet." Jacques' flippancy was followed by chuckle. "There was no one on watch. I suppose they did not think anything bad could happen to them when they were anchored not so close to shore. It was the galley that was most difficult to reach without anyone hearing. But I managed quite well, don't you think?" he chortled, and we all voiced our concurrence.

I stood up, signifying that our little meeting was over. "Now we have to decide. Do we attempt to take over the motor launch when it comes? Or do we beat a hasty retreat and hide until the authorities from Nice or some other port come looking for us? This, or any passing boat, that might drop anchor to spend a day or two here."

"We cannot possibly take the launch from them. Jacques has already told us there will be at least four coming from the yacht, and perhaps three from the launch." Jenny rose from the log she had been sitting on, her arms wide in a gesture signifying how hopeless, if not foolhardy any attempt would be.

"One vote for running," Peter gave an exaggerated sigh that clearly stated his contempt for Jenny's opinion.

"You'll miss your chance to meet David if you do," Simon giggled, followed by a wink at his brother.

I could have happily given the wee man a sharp clout where it would have hurt the most for his witticism, had Sarah not got there first.

"Och! Sarah that hurt!" Simon exclaimed rubbing the back of his head, his eyes wide in disbelief.

"Something I should have done a long while ago." Sarah said firmly.

"I'll second that," Jenny supported her friend, scowling across at her antagonist.

I waited until the situation had cooled before continuing. "What do the rest of you say?

"If you do decide on trying to take the launch, how do you intend doing it?" Sarah's eyes showed concern, and I flattered myself into thinking that most of that concern was for me.

"I don't think we need go into that just now, Sarah, let's first decide who is for or against the idea, considering that you are all involved one way or another. And please hurry, we don't have much time if we do decide to try for the launch, which Jacques is convinced will be here today."

"Do us boys get a vote, West?" Simon asked, now a polite little boy again.

I had had enough. "Right that's it. We hide our dinghy, as best we can. You, Peter, will take your brother and the girls and head a little way up the shore. When you hear the launch coming from down here, you will know we have succeeded in taking it over, so be ready all of you to climb on board. If, after awhile, you don't hear the launch coming from this direction, start making your way up the island and climb the tallest hill you can find and hide there. Is that clear?"

"So you and Jacques will try taking the launch by yourselves? Is this what you are trying to say? You don't want me? I'm not grown up enough to be of any use to you?" Peter's eyes shone with embarrassment, his face a picture of humiliation.

I understood how he must feel, I would have felt the same in his position at his age, but I could not risk the kid getting himself hurt, or even killed. These were men that he would be facing, to put it mildly, evil men with guns. I, myself, did not relish the thought. By the same token, it was quite unfair that I should feel so much concern for Peter when Jacques himself was only a couple of years older. Yet without the young French boy's help, the whole project was doomed to failure, considering I had as much chance of succeeding without him as I had of swimming home.

It was also unfair to take the boy's help for granted. So thinking this, I asked of him, while trying not to look at Peter. "What do you think, Jacques, do you think we can do it, just you and me?"

"I think we must try, Monsieur West, it might be quite some time before any ship might call to spend a day or two here. And the food I brought will not last so long."

I nodded.

"No. But the authorities will be looking for us." Jenny broke in. Sounding desperate, she went on. "We told Mister Desmond that we would be back today, Saturday, or tomorrow at the latest."

"Our Boss will not be due until Tuesday." Sarah reminded her.

"I realise this Sarah but there are bound to contact us by Mobile before that, and as there will be no answer from any of us, they are sure to get in touch with our hotel."

It was sound thinking and, in my case, I was sure Fenton would think the same. It also gave me another grain of hope that my brother was due to land early Monday.

"Ok," I conceded, "we can try it both ways. Jacques and I will try and get the launch from the bad guys, and, if we fail, you lot high tail it for the hills, as they say in the pictures."

I gave my watch a hasty glance. We had spent way too much time discussing the pros and cons of our problem.

"Throw a few more branches over our boat you lot, while Jacques and I begin Plan A." I threw each of them a look designed to defuse the situation, and with it I hoped a little of their worries. "And don't even ask what Plan B is."

My instructions over, Jacques and I prepared to move off, and I gave Sarah the thumbs up. I should have liked to have given her much more but, due to circumstances, this was the best I could do. Peter saw me do it, and I took the opportunity to wave him to me.

"Peter should things go haywire, it's up to you to keep your brother and the girls safe. If we fail, but manage to escape, we will try to find you all in amongst the higher hills, so keep a sharp lookout for us. However, we will not lead any of Shawman's men to you should they be on our heels so to speak. Remember, if things go bad for us, it will all be up to you. Use Jacques backpack to hold all the clothes you won't need during the heat of the day. Better to have something warm to wear when the sun goes down. Ok?" I held out my hand to him. "Good luck Peter, I am relying on you. I hope we will meet again soon."

Peter shook my hand and, by the look in his eyes, I saw that I had succeeded in restoring his pride with the responsibility that I had imposed on him. Then, our goodbyes said, Jacques and I left to do I knew not what, but definitely it would be our best.

Although our discussions had taken quite a while, it was still early morning, and I followed my young friend along a path to where the drugs had been hidden by Sea Horse upon its arrival.

I would never have found the place without Jacques' help; so overgrown was the entrance to what I first thought was a crack in a rock. I looked around admiringly, not only that anyone had originally found such a place, also the fact that there were no tell tale signs that anyone had been here recently.

Jacques moved a few branches away to reveal a larger opening in the rock, and stood back, with a "Voila!" and invited me to step inside.

Inside was larger than I had imagined it to be and a dozen or so bails took up most of the space.

Jacques handed me his knife and I slashed a bail open, then slit one of small packages. "Cocaine." I scowled at the sight of white powder. "It won't burn."

Jacques understood my disappointment. "Mr Shawman will make much profit from this."

He walked to where a few more bails were stored. "But these will burn Monsieur West, these are bails of Cannabis."

I heaved a sigh of relief. "So we still have a plan, eh? I'll set fire to the Cannabis, and hopefully this should give off enough smoke to have our friends running here while we try for the launch." At Jacques nod, I went on, "I think I can manage from here, Jacques, you had better find a hiding place on the off chance our friends might arrive to trap us sooner than we expect."

"Perhaps so, Monsieur West but I think as the launch will not arrive until this afternoon and I am sure it will, the crew from Sea Horse will not want to remain hidden for too long. Oui?"

"If you think so." I slit open the remaining bails and handed Jacques back his knife. "You might need this, but I sincerely hope not."

The boy took the weapon and, with a final salute, left me to play my part in this little melodrama of ours.

Now that I was alone, yet not alone, having caught sight of a few of the original denizens, spiders and creepy-crawlies, as we Scots would say, or something similar to that effect, the cave felt eerie, and I did not relish the time I would have to spend here. I tried to be friendly with a few of the inhabitants with a cheery good morning as they scurried past on their way, no doubt to their own local supermarket for creepy crawlies, and none ventured too close, so it seemed to work. I sat down on one of the bails and watched a few holding a meeting before they too departed on their way.

As I sat there, I deduced that the crew from the yacht would position themselves around the area close to where the launch would land in expectation of us attempting to take it when its crew left to come here to the cave to carry back the bails and, when we did so, they would pounce on us from their hiding places. However, if the launch's crew decided to leave one man on guard, it would make Jacques task a great deal harder when he came to tackle the man from the seaboard side. It was a lot to ask of the boy.

Perhaps, my whole idea was wrong in attempting to steal the launch and, instead, we should all have made our way to the hill at the top of the island and take our chances there of surviving until someone from the mainland came looking for us. Well, it was too late now, I said to my small companions, who were still scurrying around.

It was an island where time stood still. Several glances at my watch in what felt like three hours showed I had only been in the cave for less than one, so slowly was time passing.

About a half hour later, I heard the sound of a launch approaching and guessed it was the one Jacques and I were expecting. The sound stopped and I knew for sure that it was the one coming to pick up the drugs.

Making my way round the two Cannabis bails that I had dragged to the entrance, I took out Jacques matches that he had obtained from his raid on the yacht, thankful that he had done so as I would not have relished the idea of rubbing two sticks together. Almost immediately, the bails caught and smoke billowed up into the blue sky. It was time to leave.

My plan was to make a detour back to where the launch was anchored, and hopefully avoid any of Shawman's men who I suspected lay in wait for our attempt to take the launch. Fortunately for me, my caution worked. Suddenly, bodies appeared, from out of the undergrowth, and I recognised the cook for one, then the taller figure of David, and to my horror Cockney Joe, all had seen the smoke, and were headed in the direction of the cave.

Still cautious, I made my way through the undergrowth until I came at last in sight of the small launch. I started to run across the sand to where it was moored, when to my horror, I saw that someone was still on board and that someone was not Jacques; 'that' someone had been left to guard the boat.

Now halfway across the beach the figure could not fail to see me. I had no choice but to keep on running, the soft sand slowing my progress. Now nearing the launch I was close enough to see the figure draw the pistol from his waistband. *God*! I thought, *I've had it*!

I was much too far away do anything, also I had no chance of running back the way I had come without my adversary failing to hit me in the back.

I drew to an abrupt halt, my feet in conjunction with my brain unable to function and awaiting the fatal shot, when I saw Jacques vault on board catching my would be assassin unawares from behind. Now I knew what I had to do, and I started to the boy's aid, the feeling of relief that I was still alive and also the realisation that my plan had every chance of succeeding spurring me on.

However, my elation was only short lived, Jacques's opponent was much too strong for him, and now that he had recovered from his initial surprise, was striking the boy blow after blow, the last, sending the young Frenchman into the water.

Now my speed, such as it was, was drawing me closer to the man with the gun again. I let out what at any other time would have had folk laughing at the sound escaping from my throat, but this was no comic occasion, at least not to me, and I swung round as fast as the sand would allow and headed back the way I had come, expecting to feel the sting of a bullet in my back at any moment.

I covered a few yards more before the first shot buried itself in the sand with a plop at my feet, the second a little way ahead, and I judge that this last one had missed my head by inches. Third time unlucky, I choked, but none came, and I successfully reached the cover of the trees.

Scrambling through the undergrowth, I chanced a quick look back. Smoke billowed up into the clear blue sky, and I shuddered to think what would happen to me should I get caught. How many thousand Euros worth of drugs had Jacques and I destroyed? Then again, how many lives had we saved in doing so?

Someone was running across the sand towards me, and it wasn't Jacques. I did not wait to make his acquaintance but kept on running. There was some sort of path to my right so I headed for it, which made the going that bit easier. Already my breathing was becoming more laboured, but I dared not halt, or even slow. I left the path and snapped a look behind me and saw that there were two men chasing. Who they were I did not know nor did I care to find out. A shot rang out, hitting a tree to my right, and I dived deeper into the undergrowth, concluding that even if they did not see me they would hear my rasping breathing: in fact, the entire island would hear it.

Some distance behind to my left, someone called out what I took to be instructions on where they took me to be. I ran on, pushing and throwing everything aside that grew in my way, and wishing I had a machete to use in more ways than one.

It was inevitable that sooner or later I would have to halt to regain my breath...or some of it. My legs ached; in fact, my entire body did. I stood leaning against a tree, listening intently for any sound. I heard a lot...my pursuers were not halting. I chanced a quick look from behind my screen where a little man was headed towards me. It was the cook from Sea Horse. But no longer so little, now that he held a pistol in his hand and, by the way, he held it I was certain he knew how to use it. Presumably on me!

Another sound to my right informed me that I was all but trapped. Even should the cook pass me the other sod would still see me. I looked down and around me and cautiously picked up a small branch of a tree to use as a club. The cook had almost reached my tree, and I backed a little way around it in order to let him pass and, as he did so I struck out, catching him in the throat, and he gave a short gurgle and fell to the ground, his gun flying into the undergrowth.

I cursed, there was no way I could find the pistol before number two baddy arrived, and cursing again, (but quietly) I started to run, though not very far before the sound of a gun exploded close to my ear. Soon, I thought I am going to run out of curses for this one had me shout out involuntarily, so close and unexpected had it been.

The proximity of the shot put new life into me, and I veered off to my right. Now, a second problem presented itself, I was running out of trees and undergrowth, and the direction of my flight was taking me towards the side of a hill...*a large hill, a large barren hill*! I started for it, grasping at the first turf of grass that I came upon and levered myself over the first rise in the ground onto the other side which hid me for a time. Behind me, there was only one way to go and that was up. Below me, my adversary was almost clear of the trees. Should I start to climb he could not but fail to see me, for this side of the hill was as bare as my bank book. I shrugged. I had no time to lose. My rock would not hide me for long.

The man who was chasing me was now clear of the woods and, for a moment, stood searching for any sign of which way I might have gone. It did not take him long to decide that I had gone up instead of down, there being very little cover that way, and he would have seen me had I chosen to have done so.

Though unaware I was behind the rock, gun in hand, he started in my direction. Still using the cover of the rock, I backed away, and shot a quick look upwards, calculating on my reaching the next cluster of rocks before he knew where I was and had time to get off a shot. Taking a deep breath, I went for it, my ears cocked for the sound of a pistol shot, and darted for my second place of refuge.

I gave a little sigh of relief. I had made it to my second shelter but my hunter was drawing closer. If I veered to the right, and climbed higher, it would eventually bring me back to the woods I had just left, only a little higher up. There was, however the possibility that on doing so I might run into Shawman's other little playmates. I decided to keep on going in the direction in which I had began my climb and make for the ridge above me.

What was on the other side of the ridge I did not know. It could well be a sheer drop or a gradient similar to the one I was on. Another shot hastened my curiosity to find out.

A few further climbs brought me within a few yards of the top. Here massive boulders blocked my way but, if I could work my way around them, they would help shield me from my pursuer. I rounded one and a few strides more took me to the top. I halted and let out the strongest of my curses for the day, it was a sheer drop, and I felt dizzy just standing there looking down. I turned away. I was trapped, and rounding one of the massive boulders came my pursuer who upon seeing me, stood there grinning, pistol in hand.

"It's all over, whoever you are." He waved his gun, gesturing that he wanted me to head back down the hill. At least, he had not asked me to jump.

I had not seen this man before so I figured he was one of those who had arrived on the launch. He drew a little closer to where I stood and I saw his expression change as though a thought had just entered his mind.

"I don't suppose it will matter to the Boss, how, or where, you get it so long as you get it."

I swallowed. Perhaps, the term 'for the high jump' was about to take on a completely new meaning.

He waved the gun. "Up there. Start climbing. Or would you rather have it here?"

"Would it upset you if I said neither?" I asked flippantly.

"Wise guy." He waved his gun. "Up there."

Keeping a safe distance, he followed me to the top.

"No chance of a parachute, I suppose."

"I can see why the Boss wants to be quit of you. I would too if I had to listen to your jokes."

I smiled to myself, Simon would wholeheartedly have agreed with him.

He stood across from me, presumably to see that my fall was fatal and, out of curiosity, count how many times I bounced on the way down.

I stepped away from the ridge and a little closer to him.

"Don't try anything, motor mouth. And if you think you can bribe me into letting you go, or anything, forget it." He took a step backwards, fearing my intentions were to rush him, and why not, I was going to die anyway?

His stepping back took him closer to the massive boulder I had so recently hid behind and, close enough for me to see his expression change from one of surprise to one of realisation, when a second stone hit him on the head and he fell backwards, his gun flying from his hand. In vain, he attempted to retain his balance, but there was nothing left under his feet but open air and he fell screaming over the side.

From where I stood, I saw my antagonist body descend, arms and legs spread eagled in a manner not unlike someone in free fall, until he hit a rocky outcrop which sent him bouncing twisting and turning to the open ground below.

I took a step away from the ridge and looked across to where Jacques also stood watching the fall.

"What kept you?" I laughed, but there was no mirth attached to it. Even if the man with the gun had meant for me what had happened to him, I saw no reason to feel pleased, relief maybe but that was all. "Until I saw you from the ridge, I didn't know what had happened to you."

"It was a difficult decision for me to make, whether to let the man suffer more of your humour or come to your aid." Jacques's attempt at flippancy helped defuse the situation.

"Not you too, Jacques? Do you think I could have made any of those little witticism had I not known you were there? Certainly not when I knew what he had in store for me." I jerked a thumb at the ridge behind me. "By the way, thanks again, Jacques."

"Merci, monsieur."

Together we moved away from the ridge top.

"Where, or what, do we do now, Monsieur West?"

I pointed to a gully running parallel to the top of the hill. "I think we should make for there for a start. At least, we will be hidden from any prying eyes from below, and perhaps see without being seen."

It was just as well that we did so, for there in the distance below, three indistinct figures suddenly appeared.

"Can you make out any of them Jacques?" I asked shielding my eyes from the sun with a hand.

"No, maybe the tallest one is the man Cockney Joe. Maybe not," He shrugged his indifference.

"They're still hunting for us. I hope our little lot are well ahead of them."

"I should think so. They were some distance away from the launch when the chase started and I should think that they would remember your telling them to make for that big hill there." Jacques pointed to where the tallest hill loomed before us.

"That's the furthest we can go on this island, without falling into the sea." I said bitterly.

"Then, we too, must make for there. Perhaps, we will catch up with the boys and girls. Oui?"

"You mean before those guys down there do?"

We set off, leaving our gully to climb the rocky, but otherwise barren slope, of what I hoped would be our last hill. It was now well past midday but the heat from the sun was oppressive even at this altitude. Jacques had long since discarded his heavy polo-neck jersey, which he had tied around his waist.

I was glad my jerkin was in his backpack with our little band, and I had not to carry it, feeling weaker and hungrier at every step.

"I think I need a little rest, Jacques. Not as young as I used to be," I wheezed at him like some geriatric or Moses after forty years in the desert.

My companion nodded his understanding and sat down on a boulder while I just flopped down, content to sit there until the Big Man in the sky sent for me.

"What do you think will happen to me when this over, West?" Jacques plucked a blade of grass while he awaited my answer.

"I take it you mean when Shawman gets what's coming to him and we all return to normal and live happy ever after?"

"Oui. I mean what will happen to me? I am part of Shawman's organisation so to speak. This is my fourth trip to the island, and I have helped him smuggle the dope."

"That's a long way away, Jacques. We still have to get out of this. However, if we do, I will certainly speak on your behalf, when I will tell them how many times you have saved my life...all our lives."

"This you would do for me? Me, a thief? And you do not know what other bad things I have done."

"No, and I do not want to know. You are not a bad lad, Jacques, so let's leave it at that. Eh?"

While we resumed our trek up the side of this, the most northern and steepest hill on the island, I mulled over what Jacques had told me of himself. All of which I believed to be true.

After the death of his parents, a result of a car accident, he had become an orphan and, at the age of fifteen, had run away from the orphanage, where he had been sent, due to none of his so called kin wanting the responsibility of looking after him. Eventually, he had made his way to Nice from Paris, having existed on whatever work he could find. That was when he had met up with a gang who had put him up, until dissatisfied by his lack of contribution, had forced him into thieving for them in order to pay his way or find himself on the street once more. It was in this way that he had made the acquaintance of Shawman who had taken him on as part of the crew, but he had been unaware at that time of what type of man Shawman was, or the business he was into until it was too late. The rest, Jacques said, "you know."

Again, I halted, put a hand up to shade my eyes from the sun, and studied the climb before me. Oh, how I craved for something...anything to eat, and I was afraid that even Jacques's jersey was becoming an inviting meal. I thought of the food I had discarded at home all because it was one day over its sell by date. Now, if I had any, I would not hesitate to eat it, the wrapping included These thoughts also brought to mind my dear old mother's saying of 'You never miss the water until the well runs dry' and right now my well was really dry.

I scanned the hillside for the easiest ascent when I thought I saw a figure move, then there were two. Either, there *were* two or I was suffering from double vision. However, Jacques came to my aid. "It is the garcons...Peter and Simon!" He pointed to where I thought I had seen the figures. "I am certain it is them."

It was, and the boys had also seen us, and came scrambling down the hill to greet us.

"I knew you could make it!" Simon called out, running towards me and I wrapped my arms around him to halt his momentum.

"I didn't know you cared," I said into his upturned face,

Simon curled a lip and released himself from my hold. "Who do you think I am? Sarah?" Now he was the cheeky wee boy I knew when first we met.

"Simon," Peter scolded him while attempting not to grin at his brother's humour.

"I failed to capture the launch," Jacques said morosely.

"They were far too many of them," I explained before Jacques could continue his gloomy apology.

"Never mind, Jacques, we can always try again," Simon grinned cheerfully at him. He turned and took a few steps up the hill where he beckoned us to follow him. "Sarah and Jenny are up there." He pointed upwards.

I moaned. "Not too far, I hope. I'm whacked."

"I will help you, West," Peter put out hand to help. Gratefully, I leaned on him.

"I'll be all right when I get my breath back. At the moment, I don't know where it is but it should be back soon." I let out what I hoped would pass for a laugh,

Simon cast his eyes to the heavens his expression saying 'he's still at it with the so called jokes.'

Peter chuckled at the look. "Never mind him, Simon. He's delirious." And, continued to help me on my way,

The boys led Jacques and I to a hollow where the girls lay dozing. Sarah was the first to open her eyes. She saw me and rose. "Glad to see you both safe," she encompassed us both in a weak smile of welcome.

Immediately, I saw the change in her appearance and I cast a look at Jenny, who acknowledged my presence with a feeble wave of her hand and a nod at Jacques.

Only the boys seemed to have any life left in them. They stood above us with the sun glistening on their tanned bodies, and I wished that I had their energy.

"What do we do now?" Peter dropped down on what little grass there was, and stared at us grown ups.

I looked around me. Above was the none too gentle slope to the summit, beneath lay an open stretch of bare land all the way down to the trees.

I took a look at my watch. "I think we will be safe here, at least until tomorrow. I don't believe Mister Shawman's crew will want to spend the night out here. They too will be hungry by this time."

"Not as much as us," Jenny pouted.

I concurred, and continued. "I will keep a watch on what's happening below, just in case my theory is wrong, and they are still down there."

"We can all take turns!" Simon called out excitedly.

"Ok. Simon, you and your brother can take the next watch." I could not fail to be amazed by the wee boy's resilience after what he had gone through. I swung round at Peter's question, which was how long would their watch be, and I saw the same excitement there.

"We can make it one hour, no more, we are all pretty tired, although I could think of a better word than pretty." I joked.

"Speak for yourself, West Barns." Sarah threw her head in the air in mock disdain, brushing back her hair in a way suggesting she thought herself to have retained all of her good looks and charm despite the circumstances.

"My apologises, m'lady." I offered her a slight bow. Each appreciated the humour, and I for one was grateful that our troubles had been forgotten, even for a short time.

"Is there any point on us climbing this damned mountain?" Jenny appeared to be at the end of her endurance. "I mean," she went on. "What if we do have the strength to reach the top, there is no guarantee that we will see a yacht or something that floats lying down there on the other side. It could be days, weeks even before someone comes along." Agitatedly, she threw a small stone at nothing in particular.

"Have you any better ideas, Jenny?" Sarah challenged.

"Give ourselves up. Mister Shawman won't kill us all." Jenny's eyes shone angrily, daring any of us to contradict her.

"Maybe, *you* will be all right, you'll have your precious David to save you," Peter stormed at her.

"Easy, Peter," Sarah cautioned the boy. "Remember your manners."

Unexpectedly chastised, Peter banged himself down with a final glare at the girl he had desired so much not so long ago.

"I don't think we can give ourselves up, Jenny, especially not after what Monsieur West has done to Mr Shawman's bails of drugs."

"Thanks for cheering me up, Jacques." I pretended to sound annoyed. "But, may I remind you that it was you who supplied the matches."

Jacques gave one of those continental shrugs, with a " que sera sera."

Sarah stood up and tidied her attire, and I could not help but notice how pale she had become. "Seriously, let us look at this logically." She folder her arms and took a step, looking down at the ground in the way I had seen my school teacher do when about to present her class with a problem. "Mr and Mrs Desmond will no doubt have attempted to text the boys besides Jenny and myself by this time and, as there will have been no answer from any of us, they will have become rather worried. More so, when our hotel confirms that we have not returned from our little voyage on Mr Shawman's Sea Horse. Remember, the text that we sent them said we would be back Saturday..Sunday at the latest. So, I should surmise, knowing my employer he will no doubt have been trying to contact the yacht by now. Sarah turned to me. "Your brother? He is due any day now isn't he?"

"Monday," I said. "And you're right he will have tried to contact me as well. He also knows I went for a little jaunt on Mr Shawman's delightful yacht." I ended sadly.

"Will they be hunting for the yacht?" Simon asked eagerly. "Helicopters and that sort of thing? Oh boy, is that man in for it when they find him!"

"Find him is the word, Simon," Jacques interceded. "Remember my Boss said that he had planned to have us all lost at sea? He still expects to do so when he catches us."

Sarah unfolded her arms and sat back down. "So what is your point Jacques?"

"Just this. Mr Shawman fully expects to catch us. He has to, more so if he has already informed the Coastguard of our misfortune. Should he not find us, and the authorities discover we are still alive…"

I finished the rest for him, "And, with it goes his entire enterprise…the end of his drug running for a start. So he will not rest until he does find us. He has no alternative."

"But surely the Coastguard will find us," Peter said sourly.

"Oui, Peter, except they will not be looking for us here. To them, there will be no reason for Sea Horse to be near this island. The Boss will have been duty bound to report our loss at sea, and his failure to find us. Therefore, if the Coastguard *do* resume the search, it will not be in this direction, but where my Boss said we drowned."

"This being the case, it is possible when the Desmonds' are informed of our drowning, they will leave it at that." Sarah concluded with a shudder.

Although I concurred with what Sarah had said, my stomach took a sudden turn for the worse; and it was not from the lack of food, it was the thought that we could still find ourselves at the bottom of the sea. Somehow, however forlornly, I trusted my brother to dig deeper into our disappearances.

"So where do we go from here?" Sarah looked across at me for help.

Before I could think of a solution to our problems, Simon spoke up. "We still have the dinghy."

"Out of the mouth of babes!" Sarah threw her hands in the air in triumph or something similar. "We could give it a try. Anything is better than being chased around this island until we are caught."

"Or starve to death," Peter added.

Simultaneously, all our eyes rested on Jacques. The boy mulled over the possibilities. "It could be done. We should have to make a little detour by keeping the island between us and the Sea Horse so she does not observe our departure."

"Then, as you say, Jacques, it can be done." Sarah quickly got to her feet, her faith renewed at the prospect of our escaping after all.

"Perhaps, this is what we should have done in the first place instead of stopping at this accursed island hoping to be picked up by picnickers, or stupidly attempting to steal one of Shawman's launches."

"You are forgetting, Jenny we did so in the hope of securing the launch to continue our escape." Sarah bit back at her friend.

"Which we would have done had I not made a bottom of it," Jacques broke in.

I thought it was time I put in my penny's worth. "I think it best forgotten what has happened, rightly or wrongly, and concentrate on what we are going to do now."

"Here, here, West." The boys concurred with a nod.

"In that case what about climbing the hill tomorrow to see if there are any yachts inshore? If so, it would save us trekking all the way back to where we hid the dinghy?" Jenny, too, was on her feet, although she lacked Sarah's enthusiasm.

Peter curled a lip, "Simon and I could climb to the top, and come back and tell you all whether there are any yachts there or not." He halted to gauge our reaction, his eyes gleaming in the hope that we would find favour in his suggestion.

"We could do, Simon," Jacques looked intently at the boy, "but if we do, we will lose much time on getting back to the dinghy. You must not forget Mr Shawman will have his crew out looking for us."

I nodded. "Good point, Jacques. Let's all think it over, and make our decision in the morning."

"Early morning," Sarah emphasised firmly.

With the going down of the sun, a chill wind blew across our hill, perhaps mountain would be a better word to describe it. The girls struggled into their tops, the boys their T-shirts and Hoodies, Jacques his fisherman's jersey, and I reacquainted myself with my jerkin.

As proposed, I took the first watch and walked a little way down the hill and stretched out on a cluster of rocks, from where I could watch all below. The ground was open, so I would see, or hear anyone approaching from there. I had told the company I did not expect anyone to be down there, suspecting that Shawman's henchmen would be back on the Sea Horse gorging themselves by this time. Well, perhaps not all of them, least of all the cook, whom I strongly believed would have difficulty swallowing his own cooking due to the wallop I had given him in the throat.

I had lain there for almost a half hour when I heard a slight sound behind me, and ever the optimist I hoped Sarah had come to keep me company, instead it was Jacques who slid down beside me.

"These will help keep the hunger away. Oui?" I chuckled and took the berries. "Simon says it will probably give him the 'scoots.' What is the scoots, West?" Jacques knitted his brows in a puzzled expression.

"Diarrhoea," I laughed.

"Oh, I see " He chuckled at the thought. "Scoots, I must remember that name for the future." He rose. "I will have some sleep now. After the boys have done here, I will take my turn. Oui?"

"Oui, Jacques," I yawned and watched him leave.

I was aware of myself dozing but could do little to keep my eyes open. Jacques berries had given me a slight tummy ache and I sincerely hoped that Simon's prognoses was wrong. That was all we needed to have to halt in the middle of being chased, or worse still when out at sea in our dinghy.

I took a weary look below, then closed my eyes, and dwelt in the warm feeling of sleepiness.

Again, I was aware of someone sliding down beside me, this time it *was* Sarah.

"Falling asleep on the job?" Sarah lay down beside me, and smiled into my face.

"That's what all the lassie say." I gave her a wink.

"Don't flatter yourself, Mr West." Sarah gave me a mock scowl.

"I don't remember you having to awaken me on the beach yon night when we first landed," I said cheekily.

"Must be a figment of your imagination. I don't remember anything." She looked up at the sky, a mischievous glint in her eye. Suddenly, at the sight of this lovely girl, I did not feel so tired.

"Some holiday this has turned out to be for you, West."

I stifled a yawn. "Different, I grant you, but I'm getting a better suntan than I expected."

Sarah scratched at something on her arm. "And it's all my fault."

"How come, your fault?"

"Well if you had not met me at the café, you would not be in this jam now, as the one strawberry said to the other."

"But *you* would be." I looked at the sea in the distance, and wondered how different things would have been had Simon not gone for his swim? I wanted to tell her that I did not regret having met her, plus all the other sloppy things you say when trying to impress a girl…loved…well 'fancied.'

"It's not the way you would have wanted to spend your time or your hard earned money, I should think."

I leaned forward and kissed her. "At least, I met you."

She blushed. "Do you think we will get out of this?"

Evidently, I had embarrassed her. Perhaps she saw me as nothing other than a friend who was also in need of companionship and a little security. "You don't want me to say that I don't think we will? Do you?"

"No, I suppose not. Foolish question." We lay for a little while without speaking, content to be in one another's company. Suddenly, I heard her say. "Do you have to sell many cars to make a living and afford a holiday like this?"

"Like this?"

"You know what I mean, a holiday in Nice?"

"You mean a nice holiday in Nice?"

Sarah closed her eyes in mock despair. "No wonder Simon finds you hard to bear."

I understood very well what she meant. Somehow it was important that she should know the truth about me. I could not go on lying to her any longer.

"I'm not a car salesman, Sarah." I hesitated, while the wee voice in my head told me to go for it. "I'm what you might call a P.I. and that doesn't stand for poor invalid." I raised a hand in protest. "I work out of a wee office in North Berwick."

Sarah's eyes opened wide, in disbelief. "You mean you are trying to tell me you're a Private Investigator...like Magnum!"

"I'm hardly a Tom Sellick," I said, "and North Berwick charming though it may be, is no Hawaii."

"But you find missing people and that sort of thing?"

"Mainly that sort of thing."

"You're too modest West Barns," she chuckled, clearly amused by my confession. "Wait 'till I tell the rest of the gang."

"No!" I said louder than intended, and shot a hasty glance back at the sleeping bodies.

"I don't want any of them to know. If they were to, they would expect me to do a Bruce Willis or something and take Shawman and his entire crew on single handed. Besides, they would wonder why I had not got them out of this mess sooner."

Sarah nodded her head in understanding, leaned forward and kissed me.

All too soon my watch was over.

Chapter 6

I had not awakened the sleeping boys. At the end of my hour, I asked Jacques to take over and give the boys a longer rest, which, in a way, was unfair on the young Frenchman considering what he had gone through in one day, plus searching for some more berries for us into the bargain. Yet, should I have failed to wake up the boys at all, I don't think they would have appreciated missing the thrill of going on watch, and the responsibility of having all our lives in their hands, even if it was for just an hour. So I awakened them and let them watch for a little while.

With the first of the morning light reaching our small hollow, Jenny rose, stifling a yawn.

"No offense, Jacques, but I hope I have seen the last of your berries."

Me too, I thought, but not in the way Jenny had in mind.

"I do not take your offense, but it was the best I could do."

"No need to apologise, Jacques, if it was not for you we would all be living skeletons by now," Sarah assured him.

"Aren't all skeletons dead, Sarah?" Simon asked, in all innocence or what appeared to be, though I was a bit dubious of the crafty wee sod.

"I could go a McDonalds," Peter sighed.

"Stop thinking about food." Simon bunched his fists at his brother a wicked smile on his face.

"Hard not to," Sarah admitted. "I could murder a bowl of corn flakes."

"A cereal killer, are you, Sarah?" Simon quipped.

"Now had I said that wee man you would have throttled me." I stared at the boy pretending to be aggrieved.

"So, are Simon and me going to climb to the top of this hill or not?" Peter asked impatiently.

We all looked at one another. Jacques was the first to offer his advice. "There is a small waterfall just on the other side of that ridge, up there," he pointed. "We can drink, prepare our toilet then we can decide. Oui?"

"Prepare our toilet?" You *are* polite Jacques," Sarah chuckled at the expression, and Jacques bowed in acknowledgment.

It was a miniature waterfall that Jacques led us to, where a few of his remaining berries flourished.

"You can take these with you. It is a long way to the dinghy should you decide to go there." He plucked a few and put them in his pocket.

"No thanks," Jenny said decisively.

"You two," Sarah pointed at the boys. "First, faces washed. Do you think you are getting away looking like tramps? Do you want me fired if your folks were to see you now?"

"Oh Sarah," both boys moaned.

"We'll only get dirty again climbing this hill," Peter protested, and started to strip, while the girl still stood pointing at the small pool of water at the foot of the waterfall, her meaning clear.

I knew we were losing precious time, but I thought that the feel of fresh cool water on my body would help revive me, and was hastened by Jacques already stripped to the waist kneeling by the little pool. I did the same, so with a grunt of surrender the boys did likewise.

The water, both in and out, had in fact made me feel refreshed and, if I was not so enthusiastic as the boys, I was a wee bit more ready for the day's events, whatever they might be.

Simon stood by the pool drying himself with his T-shirt, and winked at his brother who was doing the same. "That's Peter and me all clean, now it's your turn girls."

I knew what the cheeky wee sod meant, standing there bare to the waist. "Right you two, get started. You might not have to climb all the way to the top to see the coast and the beach below. If you do, high tail it back here and tell us what you see, such as anything anchored etc. Got it?"

"Got it, West," Peter acknowledged.

"But be careful. OK," Sarah sounded concerned, and it showed. Not only guardian, I thought, but a friend into the bargain, however much a pain in the bum the boys might be at times.

"I will go with them Sarah," Jacques said. "Make sure they come to no harm."

"Thanks Jacques," Sarah said appreciatively.

My thoughts were that it was me who should have gone, after all I was a full grown man, and here I was letting three boys do my work for me. Granted, my leg would have slowed me but not sufficiently to have prevented me from doing so. However, if anyone harboured these same thoughts, they were keeping them to themselves.

"I'll walk a wee bit with you and let the lassies have a wash in private."

"That will be right, West," Peter scowled, mockingly.

I actually climbed further than I had intended, and the boys were well in front, with Jacques slowing to let me catch up when Peter came running back wildly waving his arms.

"There's a yacht down below! You can see it from over there!" Out of breath, his eyes wide with excitement, Peter pointed to his left.

Peter's excitement was contagious. I felt my heart beating faster, and not because I was running. Simon stood near the edge of the shoulder of the hill that gave a clear vision all the way to the coast, where, on the beach from this distance I took to be two adults playing with a small child, besides which stood a picnic table beneath a chequered umbrella. But most importantly, a small outboard motor boat of all things.

Peter pointed excitedly. "Look out there! A yacht! It's their yacht! We're saved!"

"I'll go and fetch Sarah and Jenny!" Simon shouted, and before he could be stopped was already on his way.

Jacques and I looked at one another. "Do you think we should let the girls come up?" the boy asked, dejectedly.

"Too late now I should think, Jacques."

Peter stared at us in disbelief. "Why should Sarah and Jenny not know about this?" He pointed at the beach.

It seemed no time at all before the girls led by a still excited Simon appeared, all tiredness gone by the boy's news.

Jenny ran a little way past me to the very edge of the shoulder. "God, at last! We made it," she gasped.

Catching her breath, Sarah looked down at the beach, then at me. "We'll be all right now? Won't we, West?"

I looked past her to where the boys were shouting and laughing, and in his excitement Simon had put his arms around Jenny and gave her a hug, all transgressions forgiven.

"What's wrong West?"

Aware that I was not sharing their enthusiasm, Sarah looked despairingly at me, pleading that I should tell her that everything was all right.

Jenny and the boys fell silent, catching the look that I had given Jacques, sensing that something was wrong.

"Look a little way down the coastline, that's Sea Horse making its way here."

Jacques carried on when I halted to let them see for themselves the white yacht sailing towards us. "They will anchor in the bay a little way from those people down there."

"So?" Jenny asked impatiently. "We can get down there before she arrives. If we hurry that is."

"Yes, West!" the boys echoed excitedly.

Sadly, I shook my head. "Sea Horse will anchor in the bay Jacques has said she will. Even if we were to reach those folk down there before they decide to leave, we would be unable to convince them of our plight before Shawman had his launch up our...well, you know what I mean."

"Then we won't try and convince them, West, we'll just take their outboard and head for their yacht, and we can radio our Dad from there!" Not to be deterred, Peter chocked with excitement.

"Or the Coastguard," Simon added eagerly.

Only for a moment, I considered the boys suggestion. I agreed that it was a gamble, but it was a gamble should we lose would also mean the death of three innocent people, one of whom was nothing more than a child.

"It won't work, boys," I said sadly.

It was their looks of disappointment and disbelief that had me thinking that they were about to ignore my advice and head down hill, when Sarah came to my aid.

"West is right, boys, we cannot risk the lives of those folk down there, especially the youngster.

Peter dug his hands into his pockets, his face a picture of gloom. "I suppose so, Sarah. I just thought it was worth a try."

"Me too." Dejected, Simon kicked out at a stone at his feet.

"So you are all for leaving it there?" Jenny's voice rose in anger. "Look!" she pointed at the beach. "We could still do it. At least give it a try!"

"You heard what West said, Jenny," Sarah firmly reminded her.

"I think we lose too much time," Jacques interceded, "we must make our way to the dinghy. Now, it is our only hope to survive. Oui?"

Jacques did not wait for an answer but started back the way we had come. Reluctantly, we all followed.

We reached the small waterfall and kneeled down to drink.

"I have to go a place." Jenny rose.

"Pity this stuff's not whisky, then we could drown our sorrows," Sarah sighed, dousing her face with water. We got up together and started after the boys.

It was not until we were at the hollow where we had spent the night that Peter, standing on top of a clump of boulders that had been our lookout the previous night, asked, "Where's Jenny?"

Sarah threw me a look, and I to Jacques , our expressions all saying the same.

"The bitch has gone for the beach!" Sarah cried out.

"Or the yacht." I added.

"I will fetch her," Jacques, turned on his heel.

"No Jacques, even if you were to catch her, you could not prevent her. And, I should say that by that time, keen eyes on Sea Horse would have spotted you. What Jenny has done has told Shawman where we are, our only hope is to make for our dinghy and the quicker the better." I started to move past the boulders and Peter jumped down beside me.

"She doesn't care, West. If she can't get those folk to help her, she thinks her precious David will. I hope she is mistaken and he treats her the same way he would us, if we get caught."

I caught the viciousness in the boy's voice, which, when all said and done, was what we all were thinking. "We won't get caught." I answered him adamantly.

"You and Jacques will fight them and so will we. Eh West?" Simon strode out beside me.

"Maybe you and your brother and Jacques will, but not me."

Simon looked up at me in astonishment, as if having watched a night's TV without hearing the 'F' word spoken. "You mean to say you would just give up?" he said incredulously.

I nodded. "I'm a coward Simon. In fact, cowards run in our family."

It took the boy a little while to figure out what I had said then, throwing his hands into the air in despair, shouted to his brother, "Peter, he's still at it with those jokes!"

"Never mind, Simon, I'll get Dad to sue him when we get back for mental cruelty or something."

"You have a way with you, West Barns." Sarah squeezed my hand in gratitude, while we hurried on.

"What?" I mocked. "You think I'm kidding?"

"We better catch up," Sarah squeezed my hand tighter. "Come on, fearty."

Although we hurried as best we could, the lack of food slowed us down.

It was another hot day, and I longed for the clear fresh air of a summer's day back home, instead of this incessant heat and humidity. I took the backpack from Jacques and hoisted it on my back. The boys had taken off their T-shirts, and I, as had Jacques too, had stripped off. At any other time, the bag would not have felt heavy with only our heavier garments in it but, in my present state, it weighed a ton.

Wearily, Sarah wiped sweat from her brow. "The boys are doing well, the poor souls although I think Simon is being bitten alive with insects, but he refuses to put on his shirt."

"It is hot," I agreed. "I think I'll be forced to put mine on shortly for I don't have a tan like those three." I was glad that I had changed into my long trousers on the yacht, even though they stuck to my legs like glue.

Sarah gave a quiet chuckle. "Not quite North Berwick weather, is it West?"

I heaved a sigh. "I'd swap it for this anytime. Oh, for a glimpse of the Bass Rock."

The girl stumbled and I caught hold of her arm. "It's time for another wee rest. Don't you think?"

We sat for a little while, mainly silent, each with their own thoughts. The boys had taken their hoodies from the backpack and draped them over their heads as protection against the burning sun, and I had given Sarah my jerkin so that she could do the same. I looked across to where Jacques sat wearing Jenny's discarded top over his head.

"What do you think has happened to Jenny?" Peter waved away some flies, breaking the silence.

I think we were all too tired to worry about poor little Jenny. I still could not bring myself to believe she was the cheery friendly girl that I had first met. When no one bothered or cared to answer, we all reluctantly got to our feet and started off again.

By late afternoon, we were all pretty whacked, the boys looking like two of the cast out of Lord of the Flies, and they were plenty of the latter around.

Jacques halted. "I think we are getting closer to where we came ashore, West." He pointed. "If we head in that direction, we will be nearer to the beach. It is from there we will find where we have left our dinghy."

A few more gallons of sweat later, we came in sight of the beach. Immediately, it brought new life to the boys who whooping with joy plunged into the clear blue water.

"Come on in, you lot, the water's beautiful!" Simon shouted and turned to splash his brother.

Jacques turned to me. "We must hurry. We have to find the dinghy and get off the island before it is dark so that I can get my bearings."

Agreeing, Sarah and I followed the boys to the shore where we kneeled down to splash the cool water on our faces.

Sarah watched the boys, splashing and swimming a little farther out, enjoying every moment, our trials and tribulations it would appear completely forgotten. "Look at them, their soaked through." She shook her head in dismay.

"They will be dry in no time in this heat, Sarah," Jacques assured her.

I took a step into the water, enjoying the cool fresh feeling of the water seeping through my light shoes and around my toes. "Come on lads, we have to get going. We still have to find our transport," I shouted to them.

Sullen faces greeted my command and, reluctantly, dripping wet, they came ashore.

"Spoil sport," Simon shot at me in passing.

"And I hope your shorts shrink and strangle you when you try to walk," I shot back.

"When we find the dinghy, Jacques, will we put to sea right away? It will be dark soon."

"Oui, Peter. So much the better. The dark will hide us from Sea Horse when we round the island. Also, it will be much cooler."

"You said we will have to make a detour by keeping the island between us and the yacht for a time. If so, how long will it take us to reach Nice or any other port?" I asked Jacques, handing out our heavy clothing from the backpack.

"Two days. Perhaps more, perhaps less," he wiggled his hand. "It will depend on the wind and currents."

"Two days?" Simon whistled his astonishment. "Two days listening to West's jokes." He rose, and started to walk away. "I think I'll take my chances and swim back."

"Ok smart hooded one and, when we pass you in our dinghy, don't even try and thumb a lift," I called out after him. Once again, our humour had returned. Or was the wee toad really serious?

A little inland from the beach, Jacques halted and pointed. "That is the place where we came ashore. The dinghy should be somewhere near here."

Walking beside me, Sarah said, "Remember, we found drinking water not far from where we hid the dinghy, we will need some if we are going to be a while at sea. But what can we carry it in if we do?"

"Jacques' backpack!" Peter offered.

Simon turned up his nose. "It's all smelly, all our dirty clothes were in it. That's if it can hold water in the first place."

"It's better than nothing, Peter." Jacques came to a sudden halt. "I think we start looking around here. I think this is where the dinghy must be."

"You could be right, Frenchie." The voice was not one of ours.

As one, we swung to the sound, where Cockney Joe, stood grinning, gun in hand.

Of all people on earth, this was one guy I did not want to meet, and I wished that I was not on this earth.

From out of the undergrowth, two more crewmen appeared, both similarly armed.

"This way." Joe waved the gun in the direction he wished us to take.

"How come you knew we would make for here?" Plainly Sarah was bitter at being thwarted on what one could call the final leg.

"Simple. We had cut off your chances of reaching anyone on the shore, such as the ones you know doubt saw earlier by anchoring in the bay, so logically the only thing left to you lot was to make back to where you had left your dinghy. The Boss is no fool."

"Or a little bird told him, such as Jenny Wren," I suggested bitterly. And I heard the deep intake of breaths from my lot.

One of our captives laughed, and Joe gave a shrug of confirmation.

It was with some surprise that we were not herded across the island to where the Sea Horse lay, but south, until we came to where the yacht's large launch was anchored. Although I for one did not relish meeting Shawman again, it was with some small relief that I realised that we were to make the great man's acquaintance, courtesy of his transport.

Forlornly, we all sat hunched together in the launch. Jacques caught my eye and I understood what was going through his mind. If we had any chance of escape, now was the time. If we could overpower these morons, we had the ideal craft in which to affect our escape. However, Joe seemed to have read our thoughts and, by his expression, it would not take much provocation for him to use the pistol he was pointing at us…if for nothing other than sheer delight.

Beside him sat the man who I believed to be Chatel, a shotgun propped between his legs.

Sarah squeezed my hand, the pressure indicating that I should not try anything foolish. I was inclined to agree.

I glanced at the boys and I was sure the same thoughts were surging through their young minds. God, I thought I hope *they* don't do anything foolish.

All too soon in the growing darkness, the riding lights of Shawman's yacht came into view and, with it, our opportunity, if ever there was one, was gone.

We all clambered off the launch on to the beach just short of Sea Horse's lowered gangway, where stood the destiny of our fate, the ever present cigar in his mouth which I should dearly have liked to have extinguished via his throat.

"Well, well," Shawman drawled, his relief and pleasure apparent.

He walked almost to the foot of the gangway, where he halted to draw on his cigar and glare at us one by one lined up on the beach. "You, folks, do not know the hassle you have given me, not to mention, loss of money." He waved to Joe and his henchmen guarding us. "Bring them on board."

The boys were the first to make their way up the gangway and disappear inside, Sarah close behind. I made to pass Joe and he offered me his very best smile. Jacques cursed and made to follow, when Shawman, standing a little above me, said very quietly, "Not him."

I turned in time to hear the shotgun go off and witness the young French boy blown backwards, most of his midriff a bloody mess.

"You bastard!" I howled.

Joe laughed at my indignation and urged me on with his gun, and I trembled all the way to the deck, not with fear that I could be next, but with rage at what had happened to the boy lying dead on the wet sand.

We were not herded into the cabin where we had first made our escape but the lounge where we had eaten our meals.

"Where's Jacques?" Sarah stared past me fully expecting to see the boy.

I shook my head in a way that I hoped would tell that the boy would not be joining us.

"So *that* was the sound I heard!" Sarah put a hand to her mouth to stifle a scream and the boys stared at me in disbelief.

Cockney Joe stood by the door, quietly amused. I held my temper and sat down, all the while thinking about poor Jacques and how many times he had saved all our lives. I also thought of all the misfortunes the boy had experienced in his short life. No one deserved to die the way he had.

A shadow fell across the open doorway and Jenny appeared carrying a tray of food.

The sight of her had me draw in a deep angry breath. "The last supper, is it Jenny?" I seethed. She did not lift her head at my question but placed the tray on a table standing in the centre of the room.

"Thirty pieces of silver, was it?" Sarah hissed.

A tear appeared at the corner of Jenny's eye.

It was then that I was aware of Joe standing aside to let Shawman enter the room. "I think you should stay honey." Shawman put a hand on Jenny's shoulder. "You are part of it after all."

Angrily, Jenny shrugged off the hand and threw herself down in the corner, carefully avoiding our eyes.

Shawman turned his attention to us, pointing at the tray of food Jenny had brought, his voice calm, in control. "Come on, you must all be pretty hungry after what you have been through. Entirely all your own fault of course."

Strangely, none of us put out a hand towards the food piled there. Less than a hour ago, we would happily have devoured what was temptingly in front us, but now no one moved.

"No one hungry?" Shawman feigned surprise. "Perhaps, after we have had a little talk, eh?" Shawman blew smoke up at the ceiling, and took his time to begin. "No doubt you will be wondering how it all began? Well, you can thank Sarah for that." He smiled at Jenny sitting in the corner studying her feet, still unable to look any of us square in the face. I also realised that she was shaking.

Sarah drew her brows together in puzzlement. Shawman looked at me and went on to explain. "Sarah had met Jenny when she was a student, and still believed her to be so when she applied for the temporary position of looking after the boys during their holidays. When, thanks to Sarah's recommendation, Jenny got the job, phase one was well on its way."

"What do you mean by phase one?" Still perplexed by the explanation, Sarah stared at her adversary.

Shawman blew smoke into the air, and turned to Jenny. "Do you want to fill them in, honey?" he smiled. Without looking up, Jenny shook her head. "Ok." Shawman took another draw at his cigar and went on. "You do not think that your little trip was done out of the goodness of my heart," he chuckled.

"You mean it was planned?" Sarah wrinkled her brows while the boys sat silent unable to follow what was going on, and I must say I felt the same.

"Yip. To let you understand, a certain Mr Desmond has a property in Florida which I dearly wished to purchase." Shawman looked at the boys. "However, that daddy of yours refused my offer...a handsome one at that, and well over market value. So, I devised a plan to have you come for a little sail with me while your daddy reconsidered."

"You mean you kidnapped them," I suggested.

Shawman shook his head. "No, the plan was simple. Jenny was to persuade you all to come on board. This also had the added bonus of getting me passed the Coastguard, although I had done this before without a hitch. However, this was a big haul I was in for this time so I did not take any chances. By the time, we met the freighter the one carrying my consignment…"

"You mean drugs," Peter said bitterly.

"If you put it like that son, yes. While this business was being carried out, you would all be fast asleep after your evening meal with its added flavour."

I had almost forgotten all about Cockney Joe until he laughed.

"When this was done," Shawman went on, "all that remained was to take a sail to this here island and have one of the crew take you all for a little trip to the other side and let you boys have a swim while the consignment was hidden, then back to dear old Nice. End of story."

"But Dad would not sell Glencoe to you if he knew you were a drug runner." Peter was adamant.

"And if he knew the boys were kidnapped by you he'd go to the police," Sarah added.

Shawman shook his head. "As I have said, had things gone to plan no one, especially the boys would ever have known why they were on board except to enjoy themselves. Of course, your Dad was aware of you being on Sea Horse because I let you cell phone him. But it was through an intermediary, who hinted that accidents could happen at sea, should he decide to refuse my even greater offer of selling Glencoe that I reckoned would have him thinking differently."

"But when Mr Desmond knew the boys were safely ashore, he certainly would have gone to the police," Sarah protested.

Again, Cockney Joe laughed, and Shawman smiled, sharing the joke. "Should he have chosen to have done so? What proof had he? I did not blackmail Desmond into giving up his estate. On the contrary, I offered him more. For their part, Sarah and the boys, and Mr West all had a wonderful time. However, my intermediary did suggest that should Desmond refuse my offer, and notify the police and drag my name into it that I could have access to his boys at anytime I chose in the future such as when they were at school, or to his wife at the supermarket etc. No, I don't think Desmond would have wanted to spend the rest of his life looking over his shoulder. However, it is all far and away too late for that now."

Here, Shawman leaned against the door frame and heaved an exaggerated sigh. "So should little Simon here not have gone for his swim, everything would have gone off fine. Now, as it is, you all have to disappear into the deep, especially since I have informed the Coastguard of your unfortunate accident a couple of days ago. However, not anywhere near where you were supposed to have drowned. You see I can not take the chance of anyone searching for you all in the original position in the off chance they might sight Sea Horse making its way from this here island and wonder what the hell we were doing here and not out searching for you all. You do not want to make me out a liar do you?"

Cockney Joe joined in his boss's mirth.

"Surely you can't be so cold hearted to the boys?" Sarah exploded.

Shawman shrugged his shoulders. "What else can I do? Unfortunately they are witness to my little business. I just can't let them walk away. And should I now choose to do so what explanation can I give the Coastguard for stating you all had drowned in the storm?"

"I'm sure Mr Desmond and you could come to some arrangement. After all, what will concern him most is to have his kids back safe and sound." I thought it was time I showed some interest in the proceedings while I tried working out some solution of my own.

"Perhaps, Mr Barns, but it is already too late, this is a chance I am not inclined to take. I have my future to consider and with it my entire empire."

"You mean killing all us kids with your poison?" Peter snapped.

"Grown ups as well!" Joe sniggered.

"So where do we go from here?" Sarah seemed to shrink into herself, as if resigned to her fate and those of the boys. "Was it really necessary to kill Jacques?"

Shawmen studied the remains of his cigar. "The French boy was part of this crew. I paid him well and he betrayed me and his captain. He cost me a fortune by destroying that last consignment."

"That was my idea," I volunteered.

Shawman nodded his agreement. "And, you will pay dearly for it Mr Barns. I believe you will truly understand your fear of the sea before I am done with you."

The way he said it sent a cold shiver up my spine and back down again, and I envisaged Marco in the sharks jaws. It would never be my good fortune to encounter vegetarian sharks...or their pals for that matter.

"I am truly sorry that you, Sarah and Peter must also die. However," he halted to glare down at Simon, "I will have no regrets for what I have in store for you little man."

Pale faced, Simon drew closer to Sarah, and I heard a deep intake of breath from Peter.

Shawman studied the roof, conjuring up his intentions for the boy. "First I will have you tied and bound. Dropped...no forget that, lowered into the sea. A few pints of blood from the galley should do the trick. Sharks can smell blood from miles away."

Beside him, Cockney Joe saw this as something hilarious. I was angry, not only at the monstrous intentions of this big man, but also at myself for being incapable of doing anything, more so at Simon's tear-filled eyes looking across at me pleading for me to do something...anything to save him from what this evil man had in store for him.

"Stop it ! Stop it!" Jenny had jumped to her feat. "This was not what I agreed when David put it to me; he said no harm would come to anyone."

"Where is your wonderful David now?" Peter sneered, though his voice shook. "Used you and thrown you aside. So much for love! Eh?"

It was the way a young boy would put it. David had made love to Jenny and connived to have her help with the plot and now that the plot, although not having gone to plan was almost over, she was to be cast aside.

Jenny stood there, her fists clenched glaring hatred at Peter. "Listen you little shit, David did not use me as you appear to think he did when you saw us that night. David is my husband!"

For a moment, we all sat silent, Jenny's heavy breathing the only sound in the room.

Shawman broke the silence with a cough. "I think we shall have Sarah and Peter, first. Joe and I will step outside while you say your last farewells."

"No, you bastard!" Jenny threw herself at Shawman.

Taken unawares, the big man reeled back against the door at the same time as I hit Cockney Joe while his attention was drawn towards his boss my blow sending him into the passageway. Screaming, Jenny tore at Shawman's face, forcing him to drop his gun to protect himself, and I dived to retrieve the weapon. He, too, scrambled out of the cabin, with Jenny all the anger, pent-up hatred and fear of the last few days, still clawing at him. Sarah quickly slammed the door shut with Jenny's screams still ringing in our ears, and Simon bunched his fists, his eyes gleaming across at me, with a yell of triumph.

"Snap out the lights, Peter," I shouted across the room to him.

For a moment or two, we had saved ourselves, though in truth we were no better off. The yacht continued on its way and we were still captives in this salon.

Gun in hand, I cautiously opened the door a fraction and peered out. The lighted passageway was empty, although from somewhere on deck the sound of Jenny's angry screams still filled the air.

"Get behind the door," I barked at them. "Peter, keep your eyes on those." I pointed with the gun to the windows running the length of our small salon on the opposite side to our door. "Let me know if someone tries coming at us from there."

Before I could stop him Peter had crossed the room and was pushing open the windows.

He swung to me. "Now if anyone tries to walk along that narrow catwalk they will have to kneel down to close the windows."

"Good thinking Peter, but get behind the door with your brother. You can watch the windows from there.

Again, I poked my head out of the door but the passageway remained empty. Up on deck, all had suddenly gone quiet.

"What do you think is happening up there?" Sarah stood a little behind me.

I shrugged. "Beats me."

"What do we do now, West?" Simon asked excitedly, clearly believing now that I had a gun we were all safe from the Tarter, Shawman and his crew.

Jenny's eyes fell short of looking me straight in the face, and I knew she was thinking the same as myself.

Sea Horse gave an unexpected roll and I presumed that we had now left the lee of the island. "Might as well finish the sandwiches,"

I suggested, although I did not feel anything like eating but I wanted to give the boys the impression that we were all safe here in the salon.

"Oh goodie!" Simon quickly crossed to the table and reached out for a plate of sandwiches. "I'm starving.

"Get behind the door, you little monkey," Peter scolded his brother. "You can eat them here. And bring me some as well." Peter's eyes remained on the row of windows, still believing he had a duty to perform.

"Will I bring some for you and Sarah, West?"

"Just do as your brother says, Simon," Sarah snapped at him.

Reluctantly, Simon crossed to the door unable to understand all the anxiety when we were all safe inside the room.

Simon was in the act of offering a sandwich to his brother when the first shot rang out, quickly followed by a second.

I drew Sarah a look. To my knowledge, the only ally we had up on deck was Jenny, and perhaps David, who was not likely to stand by and let his wife be injured or worse. If so, then it was time I gave a hand. I gave the passageway a hasty glance up and down. Sarah caught my arm. "Be careful, West, there are so many of them."

I nodded. "I know, but if there are any up there giving Shawman a rough time the least I can do is lend a hand…maybe even two. Now, get back inside and close the door behind you, and unless I return do not come out again under in any circumstances. Do you understand?"

Close to tears Sarah nodded and gave me a hasty peck on the cheek, and I turned for the stairs leading to the upper deck.

I checked my weapon which was a Berreta and held 15 rounds. None had been used. Cautiously, I crawled up the stairs lying flat when I reached the top with only my head showing for a moment to spy out what was happening on the darkened deck.

A little ahead of me, in the shadows, lay a body, and I gasped when I realised that it was Jenny. Bastards, I thought, the girl did not deserve that, even though she had betrayed us. A shot rang out and David came flying out of the cockpit, firing as he went and I saw someone who I took to be Chatel stumble on to the deck clutching his stomach. Then, David was hit, Cockney Joe firing round after round into his body.

The Cockney looked around him laughing while he reloaded. I sprang to my feet and using a life raft for cover fired at him, my shot throwing him backwards a look of sheer incredulity on his face. Partway out of the cockpit doorway, Shawman snapped a shot at me, obviously he had found another gun, and I wondered if it was he who had killed the girl. I fired back, my shot splintering the woodwork close to his head and he quickly ducked back inside.

I was so intent on firing again that I was not aware of the knife until I felt it dig deep into my right shoulder. I gasped with pain and the realisation that I had been stabbed. Above me, Steve the cook leered down at me and tugged at the knife to free it to strike again and I swung round snapping off two shots into his midriff blowing him sideways.

The effort had drained all the strength from me, and I slumped forward my cheek pressed awkwardly against the deck. I felt the pain and the life ebb out of me. I was dying. I thought of my brother and not of seeing him again. Pictures floated through my mind of our growing up together and how close we had been. My parents.

I took a deep breath and looked up. Shawman and Valleye, the captain, the latter who held a shotgun across his chest, probably the same one that had killed Jacques coming towards me. I felt like weeping. I had failed. What would happen to Sarah and the boys? Damn it that I had ever chosen my holiday here. And should I have not? Would this still be happening to them? Were they destined to make this trip?

My pistol weighted a ton as I tried to lift it to take a final shot at those two approaching heinous individuals but, once again, I failed and the gun dropped listlessly from my grasp. I thought again of Sarah and what might have been, whispered my brother's name, and knew no more.

Epilogue

"Are you going to lie there all day?"

Somewhere…very far away, it was my brother's voice that I heard. Far, and yet no so far, away.

In my darkness, I fought to find out where I was and what I was doing, if anything at all. The voice came again this time intentionally impatient. "Come on, West, I've only a few days left of my holiday. Why ask me to meet you here if you are just going to lie there?"

I knew he was baiting me, challenging me, but I was too damned tired to open my eyes. Yet I wanted to see him, be in his world once more.

He must have seen my eyes flicker for he said, "That's it pal. Come on, say hello. You can do it."

He was right…as usual. It would be too damned annoying to lie here listening to him giving me hell for being so lazy…or stupid or whatever he thought the case might be.

Slowly, I opened my eyes the way I would expect a blind man to when wondering if he had regained his eyesight after an operation. White greeted me everywhere, and I put my hand up to shade my eyes. Cautiously, I took a peek around the room as far as I was able and slowly encompassed walls and windows. I was in a hospital, the shadow by my bedside, my brother.

"Fenton," I managed through dry lips. And, slowly, my eyes began to focus on his robust figure sitting by my bedside.

He leaned forward. "A rough time, eh?" he gave me a wink, as having been privy to my ordeal.

"Pretty much." He saw me run my tongue over my lips and stood up to pour out a glass of water. "How are the others, Sarah and the boys?" I was afraid to ask, and somewhere in my bandaged body I could feel my heart beating rapidly and the pain in my shoulder increasing. I vaguely remember lying on the deck of Sea Horse, Shawman and Valleye walking purposely towards me. Then, why was I not dead? They were both armed and I couldn't move.

Fenton helped me to sit up and propped a pillow at my back, then handed me the glass of water.

"They are all right. They are safe enough. In fact, they'll be here as soon as they know you are awake. The pillow, ok? Not too much pressure on your shoulder? You took a deep one there. Blunted the knife so I believe." He chuckled highly amused by his wit. "But you're not missing anything you can't do without."

I took a sip from the glass and handed it back. "Who saved them?"

Fenton set the glass down. "The Coastguard." He made a buffer with his hands. "That girl...Sarah? She will be along to see you soon, she'll be able to fill you in better than I can as to what happened. That's if those two wee scoundrels don't tell you before her." He cocked an ear. "I think that's them outside now. Nurses must have told them it was all right for them to see you. I'll leave you to it and come back when you have all had your little chat."

My brother was right, almost immediately Simon thrust his cheery face through the partially opened door. "Can we come in, West?"

"Only if you mean to give me a relapse." I feigned my displeasure.

The head turned. "He's all right, Peter, he's back with the jokes."

Simon and Peter were followed by a tall distinguished man whom I took to be Mr Desmond, and a pretty lady that I guessed was the boys mother, the boys arranging themselves at the foot of my bed while Fenton made his excuses for leaving.

"So it is you we have to thank for saving our boys," Richard Desmond introduced himself and offered me his hand.

"Not really. I believe the Coastguard did that, though I don't remember any of it."

"You shot up those baddies, West!" Simon exclaimed, his expression saying he did not understand why I should deny it. "After all, you are a detective."

"Sarah told us," Peter admitted, awaiting my reaction with a cheeky smile.

"She exaggerates," I countered.

"Then ask her when she comes. She'll be here when she knows you're awake." Simon nodded adamantly.

"Mind your manners, Simon Desmond," his mother scolded him. She turned to me with an apologetic smile, and I motioned to her to have a seat. "We thought we had lost them when the hotel told us the girls and our sons had not returned."

"Then the police called at our hotel to inform us that there had been a drowning at sea from the Sea Horse," Richard Desmond continued.

"We were frantic with worry." Gail Desmond stared at me, certain I understood what she must have gone through at the thought of losing both sons, and her husband's secretary. "Of course, we did not know the full story."

"Jenny got killed," Simon broke in.

"And David too," Peter added, "and Mr Shawman and the captain were captured by the Coastguard."

"I made a face at them when they were being taken away," Simon chuckled. "They should have thrown them overboard."

"Simon!" his mother scolded him.

"Well," Simon scowled, "That's what they were going to do to me."

"It was quite a plot they hatched." Richard Desmond took a hostile eye off his youngest son, and turned to me. "I would have paid up, of course, had it come to that."

I knew by the way he had spoken and looked at his family that he did not want to pursue the matter.

"It turned out all right in the end," I assured him. "You have two good youngsters to thank for that."

"Oh West!" Both echoed. Although embarrassed, they were clearly pleased by what I had said.

After some small talk, and a few jokes from the boys, Richard Desmond stood up. "I think we should leave now and let Mr Barns have his rest."

Mrs Desmond also got to her feet. "You both can come back and see Mr Barns before you leave."

At my look, Richard Desmond explained. "I think a change of scene for all round would be best at this stage. I mean to take them back to the States."

"Where's the grapes for Mr Barns?" Simon's mother nudged her son.

"You ate them. Didn't you, you little toad?" Peter poked his brother in the ribs. "And I paid for half of them." He poked him harder.

"Well, I had to wait a long while to see West," Simon pouted.

"It's OK boys, but if I have a relapse it will be because of lack of fruit." I tut tutted with a shake of my head.

"Never mind, West, we'll bring you some when we call again on Friday."

"We promise, West," Simon confirmed as mother ushered both her sons out of the door.

"I'll bet there were times when you could cheerfully have let them drown," Richard Desmond offered me a smile.

"At times," I smiled back.

"Anyhow, Gail and I thank you for the return of our sons. And Sarah too, of course." He leaned forward and set a long white envelope against the water jug on the bedside cabinet. "A little something in appreciation for what you have done. It will help pay the hospital bills if nothing else" And, with a final wave of his hand, he was gone.

For a time, I sat there thinking about all that had transpired since I had met Sarah and the boys. I felt a sharp jab of pain as I reached for my glass by the bedside and I saw the white envelope. Curiosity got the better of me, and I tore it open, my eyes unable to register the sum written on the cheque. There was enough there to see me through many a divorce case as well as hunting for a few missing cats and dogs. Perhaps, I could even go up market and only take on lost pedigrees?

"You seem to have recovered pretty well." It was Sarah who expressed the opinion, leaning forward to kiss my cheek. I had not heard her come in. "Feeling better?" She sat down. "You look much healthier than when I last saw you."

"Whenever that was. Thanks."

"You had a visit from the Desmonds, I believe. I saw them leave just now. The boys thought it quite amusing me seeing you on your own." She made a face.

"They would of course."

"You are their hero, you know," she chuckled.

"I don't see why they should think that. As I remember, I was down and out when Shawman and his captain decided to finish me off." I made myself more comfortable albeit at a sharp jab of pain. "Maybe, you could fill me in as to what really happened.

Sarah gave a little shrug of her shoulders. "Not much to tell, you did most of it."

I gave her a contradictory look. "Don't think so. What really happened?"

She shrugged again. "You told me to wait in the salon until you returned. After a time, when there was silence and you had not come back, I told the boys to wait and I crept up on deck. Although it was dark, I made out Jenny lying there, and you by the side of a life raft. The knife was still sticking out of your shoulder and Shawman and the captain were walking towards you and I thought perhaps you were still alive and they meant to finish you off, so I picked up your pistol and began firing. I had never fired a gun before but my wild shots must have scared them, for they ran back to the cockpit. It was then I heard the helicopter and the voice telling us all to stay where we were. End of story."

"You saved my life," I said huskily.

"As you did ours," Sarah squeezed my hand.

"How did I get here?" I gestured at the room.

"Oh, they winched you up into the helicopter. The Coastguard brought me and the boys back. Much to their excitement, I might add," Sarah laughed.

"How did the Coastguard know we were there and not where we were supposedly to have drowned?"

Sarah sat back a little. "That was due to the family we saw picnicking yon day from the mountain. They saw Jenny suddenly appear and run to the yacht. Later, when we made the news, they recognised Sea Horse as the yacht that they saw at the island, and that there was no way it could possibly have been where Shawman said it was when we were all drowned. So suspicious they contacted the authorities." Sarah sighed. "Jenny might still be alive had she run to those folks instead of to the yacht. Of course now, we understand her reason. David, her husband, was on board. Poor Jenny," Sarah sighed again.

"Poor Jacques," I added.

"Mr Desmond has made arrangements for the burial." Sarah's tone informed me that no one had forgotten the young French boy.

"I should like to do that," I said. "and a headstone. It is the least I...we can do for the boy."

Although it might mean me having to prolong my stay in Nice, I was determined that someone should see Jacques laid to rest.

"I think we all mean to attend Jacques funeral before we leave for Florida."

I sat back and closed my eyes. My shoulder still throbbed, and I felt weak at what Sarah had just said. "And you too?"

"I still work for the Desmonds, you know." She gave me a lopsided grin. "Have to make a living somehow."

I nodded to where the envelope stood on the bedside cabinet. "Half of that, if not all of it should be yours."

"Dinnae be daft laddie, Sarah scorned. "You have earned it. Besides the Desmonds' have seen me all right. Not to mention a substantial rise."

"Put in for overtime, did you?" I smiled at her.

"I think I should go, now that your so called wit is returning." Sarah rose.

"That's it? I thought we had a thing going you and I."

She looked at me sadly. "It was good while it lasted, West, but I'm not ready for a commitment, not just yet. Of course, if you should care to spend some money on a flight to Florida…"

"To see the boys, you mean?"

She saw the humour. "Something like that." She leaned forward and kissed me on the cheek. "Take care of yourself, West Barns. See you at the funeral, if not before. My love to your brother."

After Sarah had gone, I lay back staring up at the ceiling and wondering what could have been when the door opened again.

Expecting that it was Fenton I focused my eyes on the door and immediately found myself engulfed by Simon, his arms around my neck. "Thanks West. Thanks for saving us. You will came and see us in America, won't you?"

I pushed him back gently, and I saw the tears in his eyes. "So my jokes weren't too bad after all, eh?"

He choked back a sob… "I wouldn't go so far as that."

"Ok. I'll come and see you."

"Promise?"

"Promise."

"Peter wanted to come too, but he said that you might think him a big cissy."

I laughed. "Not after what you two have gone through."

Simon was almost at the door when he gave me a final wave.

"What did the sea say to the sand, Simon?" I asked

For a moment, he stood there mystified by my question.

"Come on," I prompted him.

"I don't know? What *did* the sea say to the sand?"

"It said, I'm not coming in the now but I'll give you a wee wave."

"Peter! Peter!" Simon called out pushing the door open. "West's made a full recovery. He's at those jokes again!"

Then he too was gone, but this time somehow the room was more than empty.

The End

Printed in Poland
by Amazon Fulfillment
Poland Sp. z o.o., Wrocław

63717429R00065